Praise For *Christmas Ghost Stories*

"Mark Onpaugh's sixteen ghostly Christmas tales make the ideal read for filling cozy winter evenings with delectable shivers and chills. So pour your eggnog and settle in by the fire for a jolly haunted night!"

Janet Fitch, author, *White Oleander* and *Paint It Black*

"How do you know you're reading a Mark Onspaugh short story? I'll tell you. You'll laugh. Your skin will chill and crawl. You'll find yourself marveling that a writer can do so much so very well, all the while moving with a screenwriter's sense of pace and economy of words. But most importantly, you'll find yourself by turns surprised by love, warmed by the comforts of family, terrified by madness, and struck numb by sudden agony. Comparisons to Ray Bradbury will be, I think, inevitable…and far from out of place. Onspaugh is a gift to all lovers of the weird, and this book, a perfect sampling of his extensive range. Spend an evening this winter season with this collection and I know you'll thrill to it just as I did."

Joe McKinney, Bram Stoker Award-winning author, *Flesh Eaters* and *Inheritance*

"Reading this book is like finding blood at the bottom of your glass of egg nog. You start off with something tasty and familiar and then everything goes to hell! Mark Onspaugh has taken all that is good and holy about Christmas and turned it into something terrifying -- the way it should be!"

JW Schnarr, award-winning journalist and author, *Alice & Dorothy*

"Whether you've been naughty or nice, these stories are a welcome holiday gift. Like snowflakes, they are uniquely individual adding up to a storm of pleasure that should jingle your bells!"

Harvey Jacobs, author, *Side Effects* and *American Goliath*

"With Christmas Ghost Stories, Mark Onspaugh gives us stories full of longing, regret, and fear to while away those winter nights. There's even the occasional dash of whimsy, and the sudden hammer strike of horror waiting for when you least expect it. Onspaugh's collection runs the gamut of human emotions and will keep you enthralled until the last page is turned."

L.L. Soares, author, *Life Rage* and *Rock 'N' Roll*

Christmas Ghost Stories
a Collection of
Winter Tales

Mark Onspaugh

Dark Ride Press ◆ California

Text copyright © 2012 Mark Onspaugh

The story "A New Life" appeared in a slightly different form in THE HARROW, vol. 10, No. 12, Dec 2007.

All Rights Reserved

ISBN: 1481014420
ISBN-13: 978-1481014427

For my beautiful wife Tobey,

who has always believed…

In magic, and in me.

CONTENTS

Home for the Holidays	1
A Gift for Uncle Phineas	9
Jack Frost	23
I'm Dreaming of a White Christmas	35
The Woodcutter's Tale	41
The Ornament	49
A New Life	58
Spooked	76
The Innkeeper's Tale	98
He'll Be Coming Down the Chimney, Down	107
Santa vs Dracula	121
The Tinker's Tale	124
Christmas, the Old Way	137
The Huntsman's Tale	139
The First Christmas	153
The Three	160
Home for the Holidays, Revisited	168

HOME FOR THE HOLIDAYS

When he came to the third dead end, Charlie had to admit he was lost.

Rebecca was asleep in the passenger seat, wrapped in a thick woolen blanket, her head resting on his folded-up jacket.

Charlie watched her sleep for just a minute, the car a warm bubble in the snow-covered countryside.

"Beck," he called softly.

She roused and looked at him sleepily. "We're here?"

He smiled guiltily. "Actually, we're lost."

She straightened and looked at the large hedge blocking their way.

"This doesn't look like my parents' house," she said drily. Her blue eyes sparkled as she brushed an errant strand of blond hair out of her eyes.

She looked down at the GPS screen which the dealer had said was "state of the art" and "infallible." It was dark.

"That damn thing flickered and went out about twenty

minutes ago," Charlie said. "I was trying to do the route from memory, and…" He gestured lamely at the large hedge.

They both fiddled with the GPS, which refused to respond. They both brought out cell phones, which politely informed them they were in the land of "No Service."

Rebecca looked at him, and Charlie shrugged and grinned his slightly lopsided grin. His unruly brown hair and that smile always made her think of some character out of Mark Twain story.

It had started to get stuffy in the car, and she cracked the window to let in some fresh air. It was clean and crisp, and put her in mind of childhood Christmases filled with snow, not the hot or rainy ones of California.

Charlie was about to put the vehicle in reverse when Rebecca cocked her head. She turned down the CD player, which had been playing Nat "King" Cole's version of "A Christmas Song."

"Do you hear that?" she asked, her eyes closing as she concentrated.

Now he listened, and he heard it, as well.

Music… A waltz?

Rebecca got her hat and gloves from the glove box. Charles looked at her.

"They must have a phone we can use to call my parents. At the very least they will have better directions than…" She tapped the GPS screen, which still ignored them. Charlie grinned, then the car shuddered and was still. He tried turning the key and there was nothing, not even a click from the starter. He looked at Rebecca and she shrugged.

Rebecca got out of the car and he followed her, grabbing his own woolen hat and muffler from the backseat.

Rebecca was already edging around the tall hedge and he had visions of someone taking a shot at her, or a vicious dog charging her and…

On Christmas?

Steady, old boy, he told himself, you're not in Los Angeles, or even New York.

Lately his inner voice had started to sound like some stuffy Englishman, a character actor from those old movies, maybe. He hadn't told Rebecca, it was a little embarrassing.

They had been invited to spend Christmas with Rebecca's family in Virginia, some sleepy little burg called Denton's Mill. It was supposed to be very picturesque and lovely, and Rebecca had been very excited.

Charlie was happy to see her happy, but wasn't sure about spending the entire Christmas holiday with her folks. He was the one that suggested they make a road trip out of it, take a week for travel back and forth to Virginia, with a couple of stops at romantic B&B's. That way, he figured they'd be guaranteed a good time even if her father still treated him like the upstart who had stolen his daughter.

And indeed, they had been having a great time. So what if the GPS crapped out? And so what if the car wouldn't start? They'd call Triple A, get directions and soon he'd be getting one of Glen's too-strong handshakes and a scotch shoved in his hand.

Merry Christmas.

He rounded the hedge, where Rebecca stood and stared.

Before them stood a grand house of brick, two stories with a large ornate cupola, flanked by two great chimneys. Charlie figured the house must be well over a hundred years old, but it looked new. The place was ablaze with lanterns and candlelight, and they could see a great Christmas tree in the downstairs window.

There was a tang of wood smoke on the air, something that always reminded Charlie of summers with his family. The nostalgia the smoke brought forth was almost painful.

"I think I smell turkey," Rebecca said, "and pumpkin pie!"

They hurried on, shoes crunching in the snow, their breath steaming in white puffs.

There was no doorbell, so Charlie used a large brass knocker set in a lion's mouth.

The door opened, and a man in dressed in colonial garb answered the door. He was tall and dour, and his face showed no hint of welcome.

"Yes?"

Charlie was about to tell him about the car and the fried electrical system, when an enormously fat man in a powdered wig and luxurious clothes hurried to the door.

"Happy Christmas, my friends! Come in, come in!"

Charlie and Rebecca went in, glad to be out of the cold. From the look of things it was quite a party. A costume party, Charlie amended, because everyone was dressed as elaborately as their host. Charlie was no expert on fashion or history, but they all looked as if they had spent the afternoon signing the

Declaration of Independence.

The air was thick with the smells of wine and pipe smoke, burning pine logs and somewhere a turkey nearly ready. Charlie's mouth began to water and he hoped he wouldn't drool.

"Have you eaten? You must be starved! Jenkins, take their coats! Give them some mulled wine!"

Rebecca touched the arm of the large man and he turned, smiling at her with holiday cheer. His face was flushed and his nose was bright red, and Charlie realized he was probably drunk.

"We need to reach my father, in Denton's Mill?"

"I know the place, my dear, but no one is going there tonight." He gestured at the window with his head and she and Charlie looked.

A snowstorm had begun. Even as they looked they could hear the wind roaring outside, and there was no visibility beyond a few feet.

"You'd freeze in your carriage," he went on. "Why not celebrate Christmas Eve with us, and tomorrow we shall see you safely to Denton's Mill? That is, if that's where you really want to go." He winked at her and she laughed, and he laughed and looked at Charlie, who also laughed.

Their host, whose name was James Chesterton, had Jenkins show them to a room upstairs where dry clothes were waiting for them. Costumes, actually, with hose and breeches included for him and an array of petticoats for her. Neither of them was quite certain what everything was for, but a valet and a handmaid were also present to help them dress. Charlie demurred when offered a wig, saying he was not a land owner and didn't wish to give the wrong impression. He wondered what had inspired him to say that, but decided that he must have recalled it from some show on the History Channel.

Both Charlie and Rebecca tried reaching her parents on their cells, but neither had any power. When they asked the servants about using a telephone, they received apologies or blank looks.

When they were at last ready to go downstairs, they looked at one another and laughed.

Rebecca was dressed in silk of a midnight blue with crisp white petticoats, while Charlie was in silk of pearlescent gray with a vest of silver and black.

"You look like Scarlett O'Hara," he told her.

"I think you're about a hundred years off, sweetie."

Charlie took her in his arms and kissed her. "Well, you look beautiful."

"You look very handsome, good sir."

They grinned, and then she looked at him.

"Think he means to murder us?"

"He could have done that by leaving us outside."

"The absence of phones bothers me."

"Probably a pact they all make – no modern devices during the party."

In addition to the turkey, they could now smell roast beef and ham. Both realized they were famished.

Charlie offered Rebecca his arm, she took it, and they went

downstairs.

It was a splendid party, though Charlie had to remind himself constantly not to talk about anything anachronistic, which pretty much summed up his home life, his work as a CPA and his very existence as a male of the New Millennium.

One time when he happened to mention the History Channel, the woman he was talking to asked him if that "was on cable." When he asked her to repeat herself, she looked stricken and said she wasn't sure what this "History Channel" was he was referring to, was it a waterway in the Colonies?

Dinner was sumptuous and festive, with strange but delightful tastes and aromas. Charlie was seated across from Rebecca and couldn't get over how lovely she looked, or how well she seemed to fit in here.

After dinner, many of them gathered around the great fireplace in the main room. The fire popped and sizzled, and the flames sent shadows dancing across the walls and ceiling.

Their host stood before them.

"My friends," he said, his bright eyes twinkling in the firelight, "I thank you for warming my home with your sweet and generous spirits. Now is the time for the telling of tales, for those newest among us to regale us with a tale of ghosts or some other manner of beast or sprite." He waggled a pudgy finger at them. "And spin a lively yarn, for the best tale will receive a most excellent gift."

James Chesterton pointed at a man standing near the back. "You, sir…"

The man stepped forward, cleared his throat…

And the tales began.

A GIFT FOR UNCLE PHINEAS

When Jack O'Shea inherited the big house in upstate New York, the realtor was careful to tell him about the leaky roof over the sun porch, the big maple tree whose roots were starting to crack the driveway and the rain gutters on the south side that had fallen and lay in the unmown grass.

What he didn't tell him about was Uncle Phineas.

The house had belonged to Jack's grandfather on his father's side. Since Jack had grown up in California he only had dim memories of his grandfather, a tall and lanky man with a big laugh and a shiny silver dollar whenever he came to visit.

Jack had no memories of his Uncle Phineas, which was not surprising since Uncle Phineas had died before the Civil War and refused to travel anywhere but the confines and the grounds of the big house in upstate New York.

Unlike most ghosts, Uncle Phineas had not died a violent death. He had passed away peacefully in his sleep one fine June night.

He did not have any unresolved business.

He had no messages for his descendants, and he knew right where his bones were buried.

He was just stubborn, and refused to move on from what he knew.

Now, a ghost can do many things: they can moan and materialize, rattle chains and slam doors, throw crockery and get into all sorts of mischief.

What they can't do is chew on an apple or dine on a suckling pig. They can't enjoy a single malt whiskey or smoke their favorite pipe. It seems a bit unfair, but that is the lot for ghosts until they move on.

And Uncle Phineas refused to move on, even though every O'Shea that came and went after him would plead and beckon to Uncle Phineas as they went into the light, or climbed the golden stair, or ascended the divine ladder.

Stubborn.

So Jack and his new wife Maggie moved their curios business to Bidwell, which was a pleasant little town within a stone's throw of the big house in upstate New York.

Uncle Phineas kept to himself while his great-great-great-great-great nephew and niece-in-law moved in. He wandered the far edge of the property while they cleaned and dusted, waxed and polished.

He sat up in a high elm while they met a large truck and directed the movers. He sat by the big pond and watched the frogs while they unpacked boxes and put things in their place.

Finally, the big house was clean and furnished, and Jack and Maggie sat down to a late supper of pizza and a couple of bottles of a local beer.

Uncle Phineas knocked Jack's beer off the table.

"Oops, clumsy me," Jack said, and got a dishrag and dust pan to clean up the mess.

While he was doing this, Uncle Phineas dropped a slice of pizza on Jack's head. Jack looked at Maggie, but she was on the other side of the table.

Jack shook his head, dislodging a slice of pepperoni, and went to get the cheese out of his hair.

They ate the rest of their dinner in peace, neither one wanting to acknowledge that they seemed to have inherited a poltergeist.

Uncle Phineas snickered at the tomato sauce on Jack's collar. It's surprising the number of elderly men who become like small boys when they are haunting someone.

"Who's there?" Jack asked, rightly figuring a ghost who could laugh at you could introduce themselves.

Uncle Phineas tweaked Jack's nose and Jack yelped.

Uncle Phineas laughed, a bit like a spectral, braying donkey, then kicked over the wastebasket on his way out of the house.

Jack and Maggie went into town the next day to see the realtor. They left as Uncle Phineas was seeing if he could break any windows on the second floor with a pile of stones he'd collected. Turns out he was quite good at it.

Their realtor, Shane Ambrose, was a fat little man with an ill-fitting toupee and pants that were too tight in the waist, making his ample belly spill over like a fleshy waterfall.

The minute he saw them pull into the parking space in front, Ambrose tried to slip out the back for an early lunch, but the arm of his chair wedged in the kneehole of his desk, trapping him.

Jack and Maggie approached him, and Jack said angrily, "Why didn't you tell us about the ghost in our house?"

"What ghost?" Ambrose asked, trying to free himself from his tiger trap of a desk.

"What ghost?" Jack sputtered, "Are you asking me what ghost?"

"What I meant to say," said Ambrose, still struggling, "is that there is no such thing as ghosts, and therefore nothing that needed telling."

"I see," said Jack. "Perhaps you'd like to spend the night with us, just to put our fears to rest."

Ambrose, who had been terrorized by Uncle Phineas and had lost three expensive toupees in the process, decided to take a different tact.

"If I was a believer in ghosts, and I'm not, then I would probably believe the local legends that the presence you are talking about is an ancestor of yours," said Ambrose, at last working himself free of his traitorous desk. "My firm can hardly be held accountable for an internal family squabble."

Jack stared hard at Ambrose. "And just who is this ancestor of mine?"

"He called himself Phineas O'Shea at one point." Ambrose shuddered, because his toupee had been on fire at the time. "I checked the Hall of Records, and the only Phineas O'Shea I could find died in that house in 1806."

Jack nodded, then asked where he could find the Hall of Records.

Jack went and studied up on his family tree while Maggie did some grocery shopping and checked on getting the windows replaced.

In his genealogical research, Jack learned a few things he thought might come in handy at one point or another.

He and Maggie returned home to find the upstairs windows all smashed and a burning bag on the doorstep. Jack knew that one and covered the bag with an old towel, then took the whole mess to the trash.

Uncle Phineas's disappointment came out as an audible curse.

"Uncle Phineas!" Jack cried.

Silence.

"Show yourself, Uncle!"

Silence.

"I'm your descendant, Jack O'Shea! I just want to talk with you! My wife, that's Maggie, by the way, wants you to know that you are wel --"

Jack was interrupted by a bucket of mud being upended over his head. He sputtered and wiped his eyes, feeling a bit like Oliver Hardy.

The more he tried to talk to Uncle Phineas, the worse the old spectre behaved. So he and Maggie tried ignoring the old prankster.

For a while, it meant broken dishes and laundry thrown in the creek, hot water turned off in the shower and mud tracked across new carpet.

Then, nothing.

One day... two.

A week went by and there wasn't a peep from the troublesome ghost.

"Do you think he's gone?" Maggie asked. She whispered, even though they were in town having lunch and Uncle Phineas never left the property, as far as they could tell.

"I think so," Jack said, and they grinned and clinked glasses.

That night, they both felt amorous for the first time in days. Jack put on one of their favorite CD's and Maggie lit some candles.

It was perfect.

At least it was, until things became quite intimate, and then they both heard a chuckle.

This was too much.

"Uncle Phineas! You get out of here!" Jack yelled.

More laughter, and their favorite CD was switched to "Victory at Sea," which was weird because Jack was sure they didn't own that one.

The mood shattered, they adjourned to the kitchen for coffee while Uncle Phineas dumped the flour, sugar and olive oil into one colossal mess on the sofa.

They discussed moving, but the cost involved made it out of the question.

"It may not matter," Maggie said, "we can hardly afford replacing sheets and windows and dinner plates every week."

They agreed to use paper cups and plates for a while, and board up the windows until they could resolve the situation. By October their sweet Victorian looked like a truly haunted house, and Jack wasn't even sure the Addams Family would have wanted to live there.

November found them getting little sleep, as Uncle Phineas began practicing a variety of musical instruments in the wee hours. The instruments were all loud and he was truly awful at all of them. Jack figured he must have stolen them from nearby houses, though the electric guitar and amp must have come from town. Jack left it out in front of the music shop late one night, so Uncle Phineas moved on to knocking holes in a wall with a hammer. He was actually more musical with that.

Jack called a couple of the reality ghost hunter shows, but most had packed it in for the holidays. They were interested and told Jack they would contact him in April or May.

Jack thought he and Maggie would be on the street or in an asylum by then.

He thought of trying an exorcism, but figured it would either make Uncle Phineas laugh or make him mad. Probably both.

Jack bought a big, friendly retriever, hoping it might sense Uncle Phineas and scare him away. The dog, who they named Bitsy, was far more afraid of Uncle Phineas, who seemed delighted to have another family member to agitate. Bitsy's accidents in the living room after one of Uncle Phineas's bouts of wailing were worse than anything the old humbug could have done with condiments and cooking oil.

Having run through all the musical instruments he could think of, leaving Jack grateful that no one in the neighborhood owned a bagpipe or a didgeridoo, Uncle Phineas took to singing pub songs, some in English and others in Gaelic.

Turns out he was even worse a singer than a musician.

Jack and Maggie made discreet inquiries about sleeping pills, but Jack was afraid Uncle Phineas might prank them into an early grave.

Both he and his lovely bride had dark circles under their eyes, and both had some new gray hairs. Jack wasn't sure, but he thought that Bitsy might have some new gray hairs as well.

What could they do?

Then Jack remembered some of the things he had learned in his research. If family were the root of his problem, family might point a way to a solution.

So, for the next few days Jack made contact with his relatives in Ireland. Although his troublesome ghost of an uncle had left the Old Sod as a small boy, those in the old country were well aware of what a temperamental cuss Phineas Patrick Morgan O'Shea had been.

When Jack told them he and his wife were being haunted, most of the relatives agreed Uncle Phineas could have been just stubborn enough to remain a rude and unruly spirit.

Then Jack asked about some peculiarities he had seen in the family records, and had them confirmed. He had an idea, and made further inquiries of his relatives. After they agreed, a third cousin twice removed who was a lawyer set about getting the paperwork in order. Another cousin sought out a woman in Dublin known for her singular talents. All in all, Jack's plan would cost five thousand dollars, which was still cheaper than moving.

One night, he came home to find Maggie freeing their dog Bitsy from the elm tree where Uncle Phineas had secured the retriever with several lengths of clothesline. In spite of the snow, a pile of new sheets was burning in the flower bed.

"It's done," Jack said.

Maggie let Bitsy go and together they put out the fire before it spread to the house. Jack didn't think Uncle Phineas would let the house burn down, but didn't want to test him, either.

A couple of days later a large packing crate arrived from Dublin. The workmen left it out front and were on their way.

"Merry Christmas, Uncle Phineas!" Jack shouted.

He looked around, then saw something vaporous collect atop the crate. A specter became visible, an old man in a homespun suit with a vest and string tie. He was colorless and slightly luminous, like moonlight in heavy fog, and his large feet were bare. He lit a pipe and eyed Jack.

"Whatcha got there, nephew?"

Jack had trouble understanding the man, and figured a separation of over two hundred years could do that.

"If it's a lion I ain't a'feared," continued Uncle Phineas, puffing on his spectral pipe. "Anyone around these parts will tell you of the time what I wrestled a lion and a bear simultaneous and come out the victor."

"No lion," said Jack. He was beginning to understand the old man, like those British crime movies where you were lost for the first ten minutes or so, then you started grasping just what the hell they were saying.

Jack picked up a crowbar left by the movers (covered by his generous tip) and began to work on the packing crate. Uncle Phineas, being curious, did not interfere.

The crate was well-fashioned and it took Jack several minutes to pry off the top and one side. Something lay within, lost within copious amounts of excelsior. There was a suggestion of old wood, well cared for.

"A desk!" Uncle Phineas proclaimed. "A stout oak desk what to do your writin' and cipherin' on, and perhaps..." He made a lewd gesture Jack did not appreciate.

"Not a desk," answered Jack, and he began to pull the excelsior out and stuff it in a trash bag before it could blow all over the place.

Uncle Phineas grabbed the bag and emptied it, cackling as excelsior was caught by the breeze and spread across the yard.

Jack ignored him and soon reached his prize: a coffin.

Uncle Phineas stopped as if struck.

"You ain't gettin' me in no box, nephew. Got one of my own what is up the hill, and I ain't needin' two."

"Not yours," Jack said simply.

Jack looked beyond Uncle Phineas and smiled. "I am so

pleased you could come," he said politely, and bowed.

Uncle Phineas blew smoke in Jack's face which, although ghost smoke, was still able to make him cough. "You tetched in the head, boy? You came to *me* - you invaded *my* house!"

Before Jack could answer, a firm but feminine hand grabbed Uncle Phineas's ear and twisted. He howled. He whirled, never before having endured such an indignity.

At least, not in death.

Standing before him was a pretty but stern woman, dressed in simple clothes and bonnet. She was also a ghost, and she glared at Uncle Phineas.

"Phineas Patrick Morgan O'Shea," she exclaimed, "how dare you treat the hospitality of such a charming young man - a member of our own family - with such rude disdain!"

"Katie!" Uncle Phineas cried. "How is it you are in the colonies?" Then he whirled on Jack. "This is your doing!" he cried, his face filled with outrage.

"I invited Aunt Katie to come live with us," Jack said. "When the medium told me she had accepted, I had her mortal remains shipped here."

Aunt Katie beamed. "I rode on an aeroplane, Phineas. Oh, it was frightening but grand!"

"She should be back in Ireland," Uncle Phineas hissed to Jack, "it's what she wanted."

"Don't you speak about me like I'm not here, Phineas O'Shea. I'll not have you talk about me as though I were a troublesome hound or a door that needs to be replaced."

Uncle Phineas turned on her, and Jack could see the old specter was actually nervous.

"You wanted to be laid to rest back home," he said, "you told me."

"Not without you, you big galoot," Aunt Katie declared. "I think you shipped me off so you could do mischief. Oh, just look at this house."

"They let it come to ruin," Uncle Phineas cried, "I tried to keep it nice for company, but these kids today are lazy and --"

"I saw pictures of the house," Aunt Katie said, "and Jack and his missus did a fine job of fixin' it up before you got up to your shenanigans."

Uncle Phineas just grumbled, not being able to argue with the truth, especially when there was photographic evidence.

Aunt Katie looked at Jack. "I'm not sure we can have the house lovely again by Christmas, Jackie, but I imagine by New Year's it will be grand once again."

"That sounds wonderful, Aunt Katie," said Jack, who decided he quite liked being called "Jackie." "But we don't have any money for repairs just now."

"That is not your concern, Jackie. I am sure your uncle has several mason jars buried on the property he would be happy to share with you."

Uncle Phineas straightened up, towering over his wife by a full foot. "Now you wait just a moment, Katherine Mary Fitzpatrick O'Shea! That is my money what I squirreled away for several generations and I am the one that sees to the dispensin' of it!"

Aunt Katie took a hold of Uncle Phineas's coat and dragged him to the elm tree where Bitsy eyed them suspiciously. Aunt Katie paused, then whispered something in Uncle Phineas's ear and Jack was certain he saw the ghost blanch, something he wouldn't have thought possible.

After a moment, Uncle Phineas walked slowly up to Jack. If he had had a hat, it would be in his hands.

"Nephew... Jack... If you would get a couple of shovels I have some... gifts for you and the missus."

Jack thought Uncle Phineas looked like he might cry.

Uncle Phineas, it turned out, had buried well over two million dollars worth of gold and silver as well as rings, jewelry and paper money. Some of the paper money was of fairly recent vintage, and Jack could only assume Uncle Phineas had been robbing the previous tenants. A diamond brooch Maggie had gotten from her mother was in one of the newer jars, and Aunt Katie made Uncle Phineas get down on his knees and beg forgiveness for that one. Maggie, not being one to hold a grudge, accepted and the old ghost actually kissed her hand with relief.

Four years later, Jack, Maggie and Aunt Katie sat on the porch as Uncle Phineas chased their toddler Kelly across the lawn. The little girl shrieked with delight as Uncle Phineas appeared in front of her, and he laughed and swept her up in his arms.

"It's amazing," said Jack, "he's a changed man."

"Yes," Aunt Katie said almost dreamily, "he's become that same charming boy who stole my heart so long ago."

"I'm just amazed you got him to fall in line so quickly," said Maggie, smiling as Kelly chased Uncle Phineas while Bitsy barked and wagged her tail.

"Oh, that," said Aunt Katie, "that just comes from a wife knowing her husband. I knew my Phineas had one weakness, his Achille's heel, you might say, and I exploited it... For the good of the family, of course."

"But what did you do?" asked Jack.

"I told him if he didn't behave, we'd send for his mother," she said, and they all laughed heartily.

JACK FROST

Glenna was only five the first time she saw him.

She had seen pictures, of course, and one silly movie, but none had matched her vision of the elf that brought the icicles and hoarfrost of winter.

And she didn't believe he nipped at people's noses. That seemed a very mean thing to do and Glenna was not a mean little girl.

On that fateful day when she was five, she and her brothers had gone skating on Merrill's Pond. All the kids from Grenville went there, and it was understood that no one was to skate beyond the yellow tape the Sheriff and his deputies put out every year. That forbidden side of the pond was partially hidden by a stand of trees, and the ice over there never seemed as solid, even in the dead of winter.

But Glenna's brothers Rick and Charlie were adventurous and thought little of the warnings they got from their parents, teachers and the local constabulary.

They usually paid Glenna fifty cents to serve as lookout. If any adult came over to yell at them, they would say Glenna wandered past the yellow tape, and they, being good big brothers, had gone to rescue her. There was a clause in their sibling contract that if they were caught and Glenna got in trouble (usually no dessert and no TV for a week), then they would buy her whatever toy she fancied at the mall, as long as it wasn't over ten dollars.

Glenna had gotten a new doll and a play tea set in this fashion.

So Glenna watched for any grownups and thought about what she might want if she got in trouble. Rick and Charlie were daring each other to skate closer and closer to a particularly dicey patch of ice, where the roots of a tree were partially exposed.

Charlie called to her and she turned to see him try again to perform an axel jump. It usually meant he landed on his butt, but Glenna thought he was getting better at it. Rick was ignoring both of them, checking out something over near the exposed root.

Charlie built up speed, and leaped. He came down a little off-balance but recovered his footing, making this his first successful attempt.

Glenna applauded and looked over to see if Rick had seen the stunt.

Rick was gone.

Glenna frantically scanned their side of the pond, but he was nowhere to be seen. Charlie had also registered their older brother's disappearance and sped over to the spot where they had seen him last.

As Glenna hurried over, she happened to look down and saw a young man staring up at her through a patch of ice as clear as glass. He was in his twenties and very handsome. He had an unruly mop of brown hair that swirled in the freezing water, and his ears were oh-so-slightly pointed.

More remarkable than any of this, though, was his skin, which was the pale blue of a robin's egg.

It was a most lovely shade of blue she would think, later.

The blue young man smiled at Glenna, and winked. Then he swam off, as fast as a shark, dragging something dark behind him. She had a glimpse of Rick's red and gold muffler, and then they were gone.

Glenna knew then that Jack Frost had taken her brother. She also knew no one would believe her.

She kept quiet, except to corroborate Charlie's story that Rick had wandered over to the wrong side of the ice; Charlie had gone to fetch him and she had followed. In this way they hoped to avoid being punished. Bad enough to lose their brother, but to be chastised on top of that!

Indeed, the subject of discipline and its expressions in being grounded, no desserts or TV was ever brought up. Glenna felt a little guilty about that, but never enough to amend their story.

A search was performed, but it was clear Rick had fallen through the ice and couldn't have survived for more than a few minutes in the freezing water. It was highly possible they would recover his body in the spring thaw, but no one mentioned that to Charlie, Glenna or their mother. Such occurrences were infrequent but all too unpleasant.

Glenna hoped that Jack Frost had taken Rick off to visit the Snow Queen, or Mother Nature, or even Santa Claus. Such stories made her envious, and she considered jumping into the freezing waters of Merrill's Pond on purpose, but that seemed rude, like walking into someone's house when you hadn't been invited.

She also thought of putting a candle where Rick had gone through the ice, but her parents wouldn't let her go to the pond unless an adult was watching her. Besides, she had to believe Jack would bring him home.

As the years went by, memories of her brother grew cloudy and she forgot all about Jack Frost. At thirteen, Glenna was worried about boys and fashion and music. She was just beginning to think about whom she was becoming, and how she might want to spend her adulthood. She had a brief period of regret when she packed up her dolls, books of fairy tales and play tea sets and gave them to the Salvation Army, but soon her posters of fairies and unicorns had been replaced by teen idols and television vampires.

Her birthday fell on November 1st, and Glenna realized that this Halloween might be her last for trick-or-treating. Charlie used to go with her, but he was in high school, now, and preferred boy-girl parties to the quest for candy and treats. But she was able to convince her parents she was old enough to go out and about with her girlfriend Katie, and then attend a party up the street at Janice Patterson's house.

Katie went as a witch and Glenna was Buffy the Vampire Slayer, a show she had discovered on Hulu the previous summer. She was hoping to see Henry Sloane at the party, and being Buffy meant she could wear a pretty party outfit and not wear any gross monster makeup... although she had to admit Katie looked pretty with her velvet cat ears and cat nose and whiskers done in eyebrow pencil.

By seven o'clock it was already dark and she and Katie set out on a wide circuit that would bring them to Janice's by eight. Katie was worried what others might think of them trick-or-treating, but Glenna had that worked out: they would share their loot with the other party guests. Others might think it was silly to go out, bag in hand, but who would turn down miniature chocolate bars and popcorn balls?

The two girls strolled, not wanting to appear over-anxious, although the mood of shrieking and running children was infectious. Instead, they commented on how mature they had become, and how they would soon be in high school and then their real adult adventures would start.

Glenna breathed in the crisp air, delighting in the tangy smell of wood smoke, and the scorched vegetable smell of jack-o-lanterns which flickered on nearly every doorstep. Some favored spring and summer, but she always loved winter. Maybe it had to do with her being born in November. All she knew is that she reveled in the long, cold nights and short, crisp days.

She and Katie got separated at the McClintock house. It was a tall and dark Victorian affair, the kind of house all the children (and some adults) believed was haunted. Katie refused to go to the door, even though the porch had several merry jack-o-lanterns and a jolly paper skeleton out front. Glenna had read to Mrs. McClintock for one of her Girl Scout badges and knew there was nothing in the house but old furniture, lots of old books and several old cats. None of her prodding could get Katie to go with her. Katie said she would meet her next door at the Berson's, whose house was modern and sterile and not at all haunted-looking.

Glenna watched as Katie moved briskly down the walk and another group of little ghosts and monsters studiously avoided the big house. It made her feel sorry for Mrs. McClintock, who was a widow and couldn't help it if her house looked scary even in daylight.

Mrs. McClintock was delighted to see her. The old woman had made two dozen gingerbread men and another dozen ginger and spice cupcakes. They smelled of Halloween and Christmas, of fires in the heart and frost on the window panes. No one had come to see her, not one. When she learned that Glenna was going to a party, she wrapped everything up in a box for her to take. Glenna protested, but old Mrs. McClintock wouldn't hear otherwise. Glenna had always been kind to her, and she said she wanted to return the favor.

Glenna left, the box of cookies and cupcakes in a stout grocery bag in one hand, her pillowcase of candy in the other. She had to stick her Buffy stake in her back pocket (being careful not to stick herself), and bade Mrs. McClintock goodbye.

As she stepped out onto the porch, her eye detected a faint movement off to her right, where the wraparound porch disappeared into the darkness.

"Hello," came a voice. It was a kind-sounding voice, but Glenna knew better than to approach a stranger in the dark.

Feeling self-conscious, she moved purposefully to the stairs.

As she reached the top one, he stepped into the light of the pumpkins and a yellowish porch light.

He was dressed like someone out of a Dickens novel, the Artful Dodger, perhaps, with top hat and muffler and worn velvet gloves. For a moment she thought the muffler was red and gold, but it was a solid gray color.

His skin, though, was a pale robin's egg color, and his ears were subtly pointed.

"You're the boy from the pond," she whispered, and he bowed low.

"I'm…"

"Jack Frost," she finished, even though she knew she was being rude.

His eyes twinkled and his lips curved up into a smile. Glenna thought he was the most handsome boy she had ever seen.

"Jack Frost," he repeated, as if tasting the words and deciding they were like sweet and buttery frosting. "Yes," he continued, "I like that."

"You took my brother away," Glenna said, memory and accusation crowding into her statement.

He looked down, a little crestfallen.

"I didn't know he was your brother," he said, and she could see he felt guilty about it.

"So, bring him back."

"That's really not possible," he said, "too much time has gone by…"

Glenna figured he meant that her brother was now acclimated to the faerie world, that he would find the human world unbearable to live in.

"Will you take me to see him?"

He looked at her, and his eyes shimmered, as if each one held a tiny aurora borealis. "I want to," he said, "but you could never come back. Are you ready to leave all of this behind?"

She thought about it, and decided she wasn't, not really. There were some things in this world she really did love, and some things she wanted to try.

"Not yet… But you could come back for me."

He shook his head. "This is the one night of the year where it's cold enough for me to leave the pond and not cause suspicion with my appearance."

"I won't tell anyone."

He smiled, and she noticed his teeth looked very long, and she thought of Red Riding Hood and felt a tiny spider of panic creep down her spine.

He saw it, too, and became sad. "You're not ready, Glenna. Someday, maybe, but not today."

Then she heard Katie call to her and she turned to look. "Coming," she said.

But when she looked back, to where he had been, he was gone.

She called to him softly, not wanting to bother Mrs. McClintock, but he was gone.

It was only when she was at Janice's party and dancing with Sean Purcell that she realized he knew her name.

##

She never told anyone of her encounter on the McClintock porch, even when they found the old woman dead the next day, apparently of hypothermia. As the old woman's furnace was on and in good order, authorities were baffled, particular by the patches of frostbite on her hands and shoulders and the puncture wounds in her neck.

They did interview Glenna and she told them everything, save her conversation with Jack Frost. She knew from books and television that people never believed such things unless they saw them with their own eyes – and sometimes not even then.

Five years came and went quickly, and her memories of Jack faded in the rush of middle school and high school, dating and football games, term papers and SAT scores. Glenna acquitted herself admirably in school, and won a scholarship to Boston University, where she planned to study literature and writing.

Her first quarter went well enough, and she drove down to Grenville for Christmas, her little car loaded with gifts and laundry.

On the way to Grenville she saw the turnoff for Merrill's Pond, and took it on a whim. She hadn't really ever said goodbye to her brother Rick, had she?

The least she could do was wish him a Merry Christmas.

Truth to tell, she didn't remember him all that well. Family photos helped, but she had always been closer to Charlie, since there were only three years separating them, not five like with Rick.

The pond was deserted, it was getting near sundown and everyone was home preparing for the big day.

The pond was preternaturally silent, the only sound the crunching of her boots through the snow and her breath that steamed out before her in little white puffs. The air was so cold it actually hurt a little to breathe it in, but she did, relishing that feeling, that connection to winter.

She looked out over the white expanse of the pond, with its familiar demarcation of yellow tape. She knew local parents used Rick's death as a cautionary tale, and that few if any ever crossed that barrier.

She wished she could walk to where they lost him, but the way around the pond was impassable in the winter, and she hadn't brought any skates. Besides, skating at night on Merrill's Pond was something not even her brothers had tried.

"Hello, again."

She knew before turning who it was, and her heart leapt a bit, as if her soul mate had called to her.

Glenna turned, and there was Jack, now dressed in slacks, a turtleneck and sportscoat, something people might have worn in her father's youth.

He saw her face, and smiled awkwardly.

"I never seem to know what is appropriate attire up here."

"You look nice," she said, but he was more than that. He was handsome in a way that went beyond human, as if a force of nature or a breathtaking vista were somehow made flesh.

"Have you been waiting long?" she asked, sensing she knew the answer.

"That isn't an easy question to answer," he admitted. "Since I first saw you, a very short time for me, a long time for you. Since I realized I wasn't happy being alone? Oh, more years than you might care to count. An awful, lonely wait."

She realized then that she was going to go with him, that part of her had always known so. That her life above had been merely marking time, and waiting.

She knew they would find her car and think the worst. She thought of leaving them a note, but they would not believe it if she told them the truth. They would think she was mad, or had been coerced. Where she was going, what she would be, these were mysteries for her and her sweetheart alone. Somehow, she had known that always, as well.

They would search, and put up flyers and make impassioned pleas on the news, and they would wait with dread when the thaw came, but she wouldn't be found.

She was so happy, so excited, but the thought of what her parents and brother would endure brought tears to her eyes.

Then she knew what she must do, and he waited while she wrote a note and pinned it to the steering wheel of her car.

It read:

Dear Mom, Dad and Charlie,

Please don't be sad, I am happy, and I am safe.

I love you, Glenna

She looked into his strange and wonderful eyes, and he smiled as snowflakes tumbled and danced around them.

"Will it hurt?" she asked.

Jack Frost shook his head, then took her in his arms. He fed on her warmth, until she was cold and immobile like marble, then gave her some of his own warmth in return.

She awoke, as something like Glenna and something not, and looked into the face of Winter, of the man who ushered in the cold sleep of the world to help make way for Spring.

She looked off in the direction of her house, and silently said goodbye to her family. Perhaps one day she might see them again, watching as through a window under the ice of the pond.

Then, as the church bells heralded Christmas day, Glenna and Jack Frost slipped beneath the ice and sped away, to all the wonderful places she would now call home.

I'M DREAMING OF A WHITE CHRISTMAS

Charlie Eckles may not have been popular with animal rights activists or conservationists, but he did have the most popular show on cable.

Each week, CHARLIE VS SHARK would air from a different exotic locale, with Charlie going head-to-head with the most dangerous marine predator in the area.

It was a fight to the death and Charlie always won.

Oh, he was tough all right, and agile with knife, speargun and lances with explosive tips, but some of the fights were more a matter of clever camera work than of Charlie's being some sort of superhero of the ocean.

If an adversary proved too dangerous, the crew could administer tranquilizers or stun the animal with depth charges. Charlie would go in for the kill, and stock footage and editing would make for an incredible battle.

Of course, you can't do the same old thing week after week and expect the audience to keep tuning in, not to mention ordering those millions of dollars worth of ancillary merchandise: Charlie tee shirts, Charlie action figures and high-end scuba gear and surf fashions.

The holidays were coming and they needed a gimmick to pull in viewers. It was Charlie's idea to film a Christmas special on Christmas Island.

He had grown up in Melbourne and knew the small island territory. He had even visited for a brief time in the 90's because his girlfriend liked the name.

Charlie and his producers decided to have the support team catch a good size Shortfin Mako and release it in a lagoon for Charlie's holiday battle.

CHRISTMAS ON CHRISTMAS ISLAND, MANO A MAKO would be Charlie's first pay-per-view event. If it did well, they would make it an annual tradition.

While the site was being prepped and the mako captured, Charlie went to visit the old neighborhood in Melbourne. His folks were especially glad to see him, and made it clear they hoped he would spend Christmas at home that year.

"It's been nearly a decade since you was home, son," his father complained.

"I know, Dad, I'll see what I can do 'once the tuna's in the can'." This was one of Charlie's signature phrases on the show, and the fans loved it.

After a barbecue in his honor, Charlie and some of his mates went on to The Blue Room, a pub they had favored while in school.

Charlie tried to buy a round of drinks, but no one would

hear of it. He was a local bloke who had made good, and they wanted to celebrate his triumph.

Several beers later, Charlie excused himself and made for the men's room.

In the short hallway that housed the facilities, his way was blocked by an old aborigine man dressed in a suit and tie.

It was Daniel Gowa, the man who had taught him how to live in the outback when he was still trying to sell a nature show to the Discovery Channel called "Harmony."

That show had gone nowhere.

Charlie grinned and grabbed Daniel's hand. "Daniel, you old cobber, how are you?"

Daniel smiled but his eyes were filled with pain.

"I have had a vision, Charlie, and you are in much peril."

"Me? From who? Jealous husband, maybe?"

Daniel shook his head. "Dakuwaqa, the Shark God, Devourer of Lost Souls."

"Dakuwaqa? He's… a Fijian god, right? Little out of your jurisdiction, mate."

Daniel sighed. "He wants you to stop killing sharks for your personal gain, and work on restoring their habitat."

"Sorry, Daniel, it just won't fly. People want spectacle, not scholarship. Now, come have a beer with me."

Daniel shook his head. "He said you will die many deaths."

Charlie laughed. "Now I get it! You've been smoking the

local herb again, right? Tell your bleedin' shark god to mind his own business. Everyone gets one death… One to a customer, and mine ain't this Christmas, neither."

Daniel's eyes actually teared up, and Charlie felt bad that he had made such a joke of the old man's fears.

"You know as well as I do that a mako won't usually attack a person. It's easy-peasy, my friend. Look, why don't you come out on the boat with us, Daniel – maybe we'll even get you on camera."

Daniel looked at him, his gray eyes the color of stormy seas. "I will come, Charlie, to say 'goodbye'."

A week before Christmas the overcast sky had cleared to an unbroken field of azure. The waters around Christmas Island were clear and sparkling, and the whole day felt bright.

The crew had done a great job; they wrangled a handsome thirteen foot mako and had it secured in an artificial lagoon that was part of a small hotel and resort on Christmas Island. The shark hadn't eaten in a week and was now ravenous. They would get footage of the creature making aggressive moves toward Charlie and then assess if the animal needed to be drugged or stunned.

Everyone wanted to finish quickly and head off on their respective Christmas holidays.

Charlie stripped down to what the team called his "Tarzan look," leopard print trunks and a knife on his belt. The boat moved out to the middle of the lagoon and Charlie jumped in, followed by a photographer.

Things went wrong almost immediately, when the mako

suddenly turned in a display of uncharacteristic aggression and bit off the hand of the photographer.

Charlie saw his cameraman being savaged and made for the boat. He was very close when he saw a huge great white heading for him, a monster over twenty feet long. Charlie did a quick turn and the thing brushed past him, narrowly missing him.

Charlie turned back to the boat, and saw a man swimming nearby. At least, he thought it was a man, and then he registered that the man had the head of a shark.

Charlie felt a searing pain in his side and plunged the knife without looking, directly into the eye of the great white.

Charlie swam to the surface where Daniel watched him with sad eyes. Charlie reached for him and Daniel shook his head.

"Daniel, for God's sake, stop clowning around!"

Daniel lowered his hand and Charlie tried to grab it. His hand passed through Daniel's. Daniel then pointed, where Charlie could see his own body floating, surrounded by red water.

The shark-man surfaced near Charlie and Charlie screamed. The creature did not approach him, but said something in an ancient tongue.

"Dakuwaqa says… he says his Christmas gift to you is the first of many feasts, Charlie." With that, Daniel turned away, unable to watch.

And, as the ghost of Charlie Eckles tread the dark water, he saw the lagoon was filled with the ghosts of every shark he had ever killed, and all were hungry. They were being led by the monster great white, its one good eye blazing like that of a mad god.

Charlie soon found that even a ghost can feel agony, and that even a ghost can die more than once.

And sometimes, a ghost has a very good reason to scream.

THE WOODCUTTER'S TALE

Gustav Kline lived deep in the Black Forest in a small cottage by a stream. He was a woodcutter by trade, and made his living supplying villagers with fuel, clearing their land of dead trees and making crude but efficient furniture.

He owned a small patch of land deep in the forest, and lived in the cabin he had built as a youth just learning his trade. The cabin served him well and the work kept him busy, such that he had little time to think about things like having a wife or raising a family.

It was not that he was an ugly man, or unkind. He stood well over six feet in height and was broad at the shoulders and had hair as black as a raven's wing, save the spot near his left ear where a mishap with an axe had delivered a grievous blow many years before. There, the hair came in white as winter's first snow.

It was late December when Gustav was called upon to deliver a supply of firewood to the local inn, a place called The Red Lion.

The Innkeeper was a stout and jolly man named Helmut,

and Gustav knew him well. They had been friends since they were boys. Helmut invited Gustav to share a meal with him, his wife Gerta, his daughter Dorothea and two men who had come to the inn separately, Jürgen the Huntsman and Anders the Tinker. These last were also known to Gustav, for it was a tiny village and they were all men in their late twenties who had fished the same streams and hiked the same hills lo these many years.

Gustav was a quiet man, and not one to join large groups. Truth to tell, he was a shy man and any gathering over two made him nervous.

"Me dear fellow," Helmut protested, "it is Christmas Eve. Surely you would rather enjoy it with friends here in my inn than your dark and lonely cottage!"

Gustav thought his cottage anything but dark or lonely, but he was polite as well as shy. He sat down to a hearty meal of lentil soup, sausage and good coarse bread, washed down with ale Helmut had brought in from the town of Kleiderhöln.

Gustav had to admit he enjoyed himself. He drank more than he should and laughed more than he had in years.

With cries of "Happy Christmas" ringing in his ears, he got somewhat unsteadily into his wagon and bade his horse take him home.

It was a quiet night. Storm clouds had cleared during the course of their meal and now stars shone like distant lights over the snow and black sentries of pine.

Gustav patted himself to stay warm and thought of how happy Helmut was. Though it was not an exciting life, he was happy with Gerta and Dorothea.

For the first time in many years he wondered at his solitude, at how he could think such a life was good for a man.

He was not a superstitious soul, but he looked up into the Christmas sky and said quietly, "I wonder if I might find someone to pass my Christmases with, someone who might help make a home with me, and help me find those things I have denied myself."

He tipped his hat to the brightest star, then laughed at his foolishness. A few more ales and he would be seeking pixies and sprites in the woods.

Gustav was two miles from his cottage when he heard the wolf. Wolves were not uncommon in the Black Forest, but they tended to hunt in the distant reaches and leave men alone.

The wolf howled again and Gustav now could tell that the animal was alone and in pain.

Gustav hated to think of a creature suffering on tonight of all nights, and brought his wagon to a halt. He grabbed his rifle, meaning to put the animal out of its misery.

The moon was rising, nearly full, and it gave everything a spectral, silvery quality. The only sounds were Gustav's low breathing, and an occasional whimper coming from his left.

Moving cautiously, he stepped into a glade enrobed in the whitest snow.

There, its front paw caught in a trap, was a white wolf.

Gustav had never seen a white wolf. There was a legend that such creatures were lucky, that they granted wishes, but he had never believed that nonsense.

The creature watched him as he entered the clearing, and

he thought he saw intelligence in those eyes.

It knows what a gun is, he thought.

The animal was truly beautiful, its white fur actually turning to silver at its paws and the tip of its tail. It pained him to think of some trapper using this magnificent creature's fur for a hat and coat.

Gustav looked at the wolf, which regarded him silently.

"Hello," Gustav said.

The wolf watched him.

So much for animals talking on Christmas Eve, he thought.

"I will make you a deal, wolf," he continued. "If you promise not to bite me, I will try and free your leg from that trap."

The wolf made no sound, just watched him as he approached.

Gustav put out a hand slowly, and the wolf sniffed it but made no aggressive move.

Gustav moved closer, and the creature did not growl or bare its teeth.

The trap was a cruel thing of iron, similar to the design of a bear trap but smaller. It had been hidden under leaves and a dusting of snow.

The wolf's leg was bleeding, but the leg seemed unbroken.

Gustav muttered a quick prayer to whatever god looks after fools, then gripped the jaws of the trap.

He was one of the strongest men in the village, but the trap was strong and would not yield. His efforts made the teeth of the trap grip the wolf tighter and it whimpered but did not lash out. It seemed to understand he wanted to help.

Such a gentle creature so cruelly caught! That made him angry and Gustav channeled that anger into his efforts. He strained, his muscles bunching like thick cables in his arms.

At last, with a squeak, Gustav forced the trap open enough for the wolf to pull its paw out. Once it was clear, Gustav let the trap close again.

He expected the wolf to run, but it looked at him and then lunged. He tried to throw up a hand to protect his face, but the wolf was faster.

It licked his face, then bounded off into the depths of the woods.

With wonder, Gustav felt the wetness on his face, already growing cold in the winter chill.

He removed the trap from its peg and took the trap with him. Hunting game for food was one thing. Trapping for profit quite another.

He went home, and collapsed on his bed into a deep and dreamless sleep, thinking perhaps he heard one joyful howl before the night closed in.

When he awoke, he made a simple breakfast and then examined the trap.

He saw now that most of the trap was iron, but the teeth of it were covered in silver. Struck into the iron were curious runes and symbols, their meaning lost to the Woodcutter.

It seemed his poacher might fancy himself some sort of sorcerer, and this made his blood run cold.

Who would craft such a device, and what did they hope to catch?

It was Christmas day and he had no work to do, so he went to the village, checking to see if Helmut or anyone else knew who was trapping in his woods.

Helmut recalled a stranger who had come to town not three days before, a bald man with a patch over one eye. The stranger had asked Helmut if any fur trappers worked in the area. Gustav told him to keep an eye out for the fellow and his friend agreed.

He saw Jürgen the Huntsman at a table far in the back and asked him about poachers. Jürgen was very protective of the animals in the Black Forest. Indeed, there were those who felt he was more comfortable among animals than people. Gustav understood this, often feeling more comfortable among trees than his neighbors.

At his description of the trap, Jürgen grew angry.

"Sorcery!" he spat. "I have seen too many creatures sacrificed by these blackguards; my own sister lost a black cat when she was but a child."

Jürgen motioned at him with his stein. "Mark me well, Gustav, if you find this charlatan or his cadre, leave them to me."

Gustav nodded, then said, "You are formidable, Jürgen, it is true. Still, even one adept with bow and cudgel may find an ally with an axe a good thing to have."

Jürgen laughed and they clinked their steins, and Helmut refilled them, wanting to be in on the joke.

That led to many toasts and stories, with the complement

around the table changing like a ceaseless tide.

It was twilight on Christmas Day when Gustav finally decided he must go home. Once again, he was a bit unsteady on his wagon, but his horse knew the way.

He listened for the wolf, but heard nothing, and found he was disappointed that he would probably not see the creature again.

He wondered what it might be like to move like smoke through the forest, taking what you needed and preserving a balance older than the trees.

He chuckled. Such talk was more the province of Jürgen the Huntsman than his.

Perhaps he was a hunter as well as a woodcutter, a voice inside him said.

He breathed in the cold air, thinking of a warm fire and perhaps some leftover stew. It had been a good day, but now it would end with him alone, as it always did.

He was surprised to find someone waiting for him. The stranger's features were hidden by a red cloak and hood.

"Good evening," said Gustav as he dismounted.

"Good evening to you, Gustav Kline, and Happy Christmas."

"Do I know you?"

The stranger swept back the hood and revealed a woman in her twenties, with lustrous blond hair and large green eyes. She was the most beautiful woman he had ever seen.

"I am called Elsbeth," she said, "and I owe you a great

debt."

"I don't know how that could be, as we have never --"

He stopped, because she was holding up her left arm, which was bandaged.

Gustav cocked his head. "How did you come to be injured?"

"By the trap you saved me from, Gustav Kline."

Gustav shook his head in disbelief. He had heard tales of were-creatures and shape-shifters, of course. Who in this benighted forest had not? But for such a lovely and seemingly intelligent woman as this to accept such nonsense seemed unthinkable.

She smiled at him, and her teeth were white and even, her lips generous and red.

"You do not believe me. That is all right." She smiled at him, and again he was caught up in the beauty of her eyes, and of the hint of something wild in them. She took his hand, and hers was soft and very warm. "You are a good man, Gustav, a kind man. I have seen that you live alone and it reminds me that I too, am alone. I wonder if I might buy you supper at the inn?"

And so Gustav Kline did not spend his Christmas alone, but in the company of the woman who would one day become his wife.

And as to the rest of their story, that is a tale for another time. I can tell you that the white wolf still roams the Black Forest, but she does not roam alone. A dark wolf runs by her side, one with a blaze of white fur near its left ear.

THE ORNAMENT

Erica Pierce stared at the Christmas ornament on the countertop with a dubious look.

It was a hand-blown apple, exceedingly delicate, with just a subtle hint of red in the fruit and green and gold in the two stylized leaves.

It was exquisite, and brand new it would easily be worth a hundred and twenty pounds.

Erica was quite sure it was worth many times that.

The shopkeeper, a dull-looking boy with bad skin, kept glancing at his cell phone, obviously interested in continuing a conversation with some similarly inclined dullard elsewhere.

She had spotted the ornament yesterday when the boy's parents were running the shop, and had placed it on hold, knowing they had their dim progeny run the place on Mondays.

"How old is it?" asked Erica, already knowing the answer.

"It's quite old," the boy said. "Maybe a hundred years or so?"

Only about four hundred years off, she thought. Twit.

"And the price?"

He looked at her, exasperated because a large tag was affixed to the ornament. "Fifty quid," he said, as if she were the idiot.

She could have taken the ornament, knowing what she did, and made a spectacular purchase. But his whole demeanor irked her, as well as the ignorance of his shopkeeper parents, who had no business selling such a treasure for such a meager price.

She fixed him with a steely gaze, and was gratified to see him take a slight step back.

"Young man, are you trying to cheat me?"

"No, I… I mean, we wouldn't."

"Are you aware that glass blowing wasn't even invented a hundred years ago?"

"Really? I thought…"

"You thought you'd take advantage of a widow her first Christmas alone. You thought you and your family would share a hearty laugh at my expense."

"Lady… Mum…"

"I have a good mind to fetch a constable. I'm sure such scandalous business practices will require him to close you down, perhaps shutter this establishment permanently."

The thought of such a dire turn of events on his watch terrified the boy. Although his father had given him a strict "no haggling" lecture, all that was forgotten in a parade of dreadful images of the shop padlocked and his parents in prison.

"Please, what do you think is a fair price?"

She made a show of thinking, then said, "Twenty-five pounds would be the asking price, but I am willing to pay thirty, it being Christmas… and I like to support local businesses."

She thought she might be laying it on a bit thick, but he lapped it up gratefully.

The young man wrapped up the ornament quickly, wanting the whole exchange behind him. He almost dropped it and she bit her tongue, lest the stream of invectives wanting to escape from her mouth spoil the transaction.

He threw in a silver letter opener she had had her eye on, not priceless like the ornament, but not worthless, either.

She maintained her composure all the way down High Street, but did giggle several times over her tea at Bale & Beckworth.

Such a stupid, stupid boy!

##

"It is very pretty," said Pamela Kensington-Smythe, somewhat dubiously. "How much did you pay for it, again?"

The ornament now hung suspended from a bit of velvet ribbon under a bell jar.

"Thirty pounds," said Erica, grinning.

"Well, it's a cheery enough little ornament, Erica, but I believe I have seen their like at Marks and Spencer for fifteen pounds."

"Really?" asked Erica, triumph glittering in her eyes and smile. "Do you see this little mark between the leaves?

Pamela peered at it. Truth was, she was rather bored with the topic and Erica did go on so. But she did serve the most wonderful little Russian cakes with tea, and Pamela wondered just how soon tea would be. "I see it," she said, though she didn't.

"That," said Erica, as if she were a matador delivering the coup de grace, "is the mark of King Henry VIII, reserved for the gifts he gave his wives. This particular gift went to Anne Boleyn on their last Christmas together…" Erica paused for a moment. "in 1536."

Pamela looked at her. "Really?" she said, and regarded the ornament with a sort of reverence.

"Lord Gifflesford is coming round tomorrow to authenticate it."

"Jeremy Gifflesford?"

"*Lord* Gifflesford," Erica corrected.

"Oh, Erica, he is one of the most eligible men in Britain!"

"He's a frightful bore," said Erica, "but he is the foremost authority on the reign of Henry VIII."

"Do you… do you think I might meet him?" Pamela asked, already picturing herself and Jeremy meeting William and Kate for tea.

"He is only here for the authentication, dear, but he will be here for my annual Christmas dinner."

"Erica, dear Erica…"

"Rest assured, Pamela, I will make sure you are seated next to him at dinner," said Erica, who had no such intention.

Pamela was so excited that she hardly noticed when the

tea was served, though the cakes brought her around.

Later, Erica came down to look at the ornament before going up to bed. Her late husband John had thought her fascination with artifacts was silly. "Baubles and trinkets," he would say dismissively when she would point out some item at Sotheby's.

Well, now she had something extraordinary, perhaps even priceless.

She thought she would show the ornament off at her Christmas party, then loan it to the British Museum. Yes, a tasteful but informative display with a brass plaque reading, "On loan from the collection of Erica Pierce." Then hundreds would see the ornament and know that it was hers. Perhaps the royal family would want it, and offer her a peerage. Or a peer might see it and wish to meet her. The possibilities were endless.

With that happy thought, she went up to bed.

#

Her first thought was that John had broken a water goblet and was ringing for the maid, then she remembered he was dead.

She opened her eyes and listened.

Ting, ting

Who was making that infernal racket? Hadn't the housekeeper gone home?

Since John was gone, she had to dismiss the full-time staff. She hoped the ornament might turn this sorry situation around, so…

Ting, ting

Now she felt frightened – someone must be in the house!

She reached for the phone, intent on calling the police.

Ting, ting

What was that sound? It seemed familiar, like…

Like a fork striking a wine glass, a call for a toast…

The ornament!

Erica was sure it was the husband and wife who owned the curio shoppe, or maybe their slugabed of a son.

This made Erica angry, for she was sure they meant to cheat her from a chance to better herself and her situation. She grabbed a poker from the fireplace and padded downstairs, all fearful thoughts banished from her mind.

The first thing she saw was the bell jar smashed to pieces in the entryway. The ornament, now vulnerable, still swung on its velvet ribbon, a priceless pendulum. On the small table next to it lay the silver letter opener. She supposed the intruder had used this to make the crystalline peal that had brought her down.

There seemed to be no one about, but she did call out, "Hello? Is there anyone there?", her voice sounding quite small and yet too loud in the big house.

There was only silence.

Erica bent toward the ornament, and was relieved to see it was undamaged. It would be worth a great deal even if cracked, but she felt that might reflect on her, somehow.

She detected movement, and thought at first it was herself, reflected in the reddish orb.

No, she stayed very still and yet something moved within the glass.

Sneaking a look behind her, she bent down and peered at it.

A face looked back at her, a young woman's face, and Erica's eyes widened.

Then there was movement behind her and she turned as the ghostly executioner was swinging his great axe up for the killing stroke…

# #

Jeremy Gifflesford prided himself on punctuality, and knocked on Erica Pierce's front door at precisely one o'clock the next day.

A most beguiling beauty answered the door, her eyes dark and mischievous, her hair a lustrous black.

"Hello," she said, sweetly, "you must be Lord Gifflesford."

"I am, my dear."

"Won't you come in?"

The young woman made a quaint curtsey and Jeremy found himself quite taken with her.

"I am Erica's niece Anne, I have been away at school in France, and only just arrived on holiday."

Jeremy gave a little bow.

She went on, "Auntie has gone shopping, but asked that I show you the ornament."

Jeremy was deciding this day was improving

exponentially by the moment. Erica was a tiresome old thing who love to prattle on and on about her favorite subjects: herself and her possessions.

Anne gestured to a glass apple suspended from a velvet ribbon.

When Jeremy did not look at it right away, she turned to find him staring, and blushed.

"Lord Gifflesford, you're staring at me."

"Oh! I am frightfully sorry! It's just… have we met, before?"

"No, I am quite sure I would have remembered you."

Now it was his turn to blush. "You didn't attend one of my lectures on Henry VIII?"

"No, but I have heard of your lectures. I am told you are such a wonderful speaker that I would feel as if I had lived in those times."

Jeremy tutted modestly, wondering if it would be too forward to ask her to tea. He decided he would give his pronouncement on the ornament, then do so.

For a moment, his eyes widened as he took in the delicate shape and coloring, the distinctive and tiny crest between the leaves.

Then he saw movement, and the face within, and his excitement dwindled.

"Something the matter, your lordship?"

Jeremy looked at her for a moment, trying to discern whether she was making a fool of him. She returned his gaze, and he found himself almost overwhelmed by her beauty.

"Oh, I just thought this was… anyway, it's clever copy, but clearly modern."

"Really?"

"Yes – you see, there's a hologram of your aunt inside."

"Why, so there is!"

"I don't know why she approved this image of herself. Really, she looks like she's screaming , and it makes a perfectly dreadful Christmas ornament."

A NEW LIFE

It was in the paper, as Jeff had figured.

TODDLER KILLED IN HIT AND RUN.

He was at the bus station, a ticket for Vegas already tucked in his pocket. Jeff sipped a double latte from some Starbucks knockoff and looked for anything that might point to him.

He was lucky; the only real description was of a white van with the markings of some former business barely visible. That van was, by now, a smoking pile of debris ten blocks from the bus station. Even though his fingerprints weren't on record, he wasn't taking any chances.

TODDLER KILLED IN HIT AND RUN.

Jeff objected to the term "toddler" in the article. It seemed overly sentimental, almost sensationalistic. No one would deny that the death of such a young child was a tragedy, but to evoke the cute antics of a toddler seemed out of place in a prestigious paper like The Times. He also took exception to the fact that the word "accident" was missing from the headline, as if to make the reader question whether there had been intention or not.

It was true he had been drinking the day of the accident, but only a little... Hell, there were a lot of people who drank a whole lot more on Christmas day. And he had plenty of reason to feel blue. Cheryl had left him just five months prior for a man she had met in her dance class, and he found it hard to be alone, especially at this time of year. On top of that, his wages from Green Time nursery weren't enough for the Santa Monica condo they shared, so he had to move into a much cheaper apartment in Canoga Park. He hated the freaking Valley, with its smog and oppressive summer heat, its areas of desperate gentrification bordered by poverty, drugs and ignorance.

Jeff had bought the van from some senior for $500, which was money he didn't have. He planned to start a landscaping business, using his experience and contacts at Green Time. He had most of the equipment already; lawnmower, leaf blower, edger and rake, and he planned to help himself to plants at one of Green Time's competitors over in Van Nuys. With the overhead he'd save, he could afford to buy the larger trees and supplies from Green Time. Eventually he'd be in the black and could afford to be 100% legit. He still hadn't made up his mind whether or not to eventually repay the competing nursery. Even if he did it anonymously, it seemed like asking to get caught.

Once his landscaping business was established and he had others to do the grunt work, he would begin writing again. He was a pretty good playwright, and there were plenty of theaters in the Valley and in West L.A. looking for material.

Of course, everything was on hold because of the winter rains. The Valley might not get snow, but some years there was plenty of cold weather and rain. Hard to get a landscaping business going in such weather. He just needed to be patient until spring.

He had expected to spend Christmas day stoned and drunk in front of the TV. "It's a Wonderful Life", Charlie Brown and all that garbage.

He had been surprised by a call from his sister Melanie, who had remembered that he and Cheryl always made a big deal about Christmas. The last thing he really wanted was to see family, especially since he would have to be on his best behavior, but she talked him into it with a promise of tasty leftovers and a present from his nephews he would "really love."

Melanie and her family had moved to San Luis Obispo, which meant a four hour drive for him. Kind of a drag, but he guessed it was better than eating pizza and watching the Twilight Zone. His sister was an excellent cook and they always had ham *and* turkey. One year her husband Ray had even sprung for filet mignons. He and Cheryl had been really tight, then, and it was probably the best Christmas he had had since being a kid.

He needed to leave before eleven to get there on time, and he also had to stop and find some gifts. Just some token stuff would do, they knew he didn't have much money to spare.

He grabbed some breakfast at McDonald's and then stopped at a liquor store for a bottle of wine. He got a pretty good deal on holiday pack of Bailey's, and the owner of the place told him that Toys "R" Us was open until noon. If he hurried, he could get something his nephews might really like. At the last moment, he bought himself a couple of Mickey's Bigmouths for the road.

Just to loosen up a little.

He drank part of the Mickey's on the way to the toy store,

and was relieved that they weren't too busy. The merchandise was picked over, and what little was left in disarray, but he found a couple of action figures on sale he thought they might like. For another buck he got them gift wrapped – score!

Jeff left the parking lot feeling good, maybe for the first time since Cheryl left. He was pretty sure he could make the landscaping business work, and eventually he could quit Green Time. He envisioned himself with a fleet of trucks – all new – and him in some plush office designing landscaping and meeting with clients while his employees went out and did the grunt work. He'd get a condo in Santa Monica – no, Marina del Rey – and he'd meet some woman who'd make Cheryl look like a total loser.

Jeff was heading east on Saticoy, enjoying his beer when this song came on that he really hated. That song with the woman who shrieks all the lyrics – Jesus, she hurt his ears. He put the beer in the cup holder and tried to find something else.

He saw a flash of something brown and orange in front of him, and then there was a soft *whumph*, almost inaudible over the static between stations.

He started to slow, and saw a stuffed bear in the side mirror. He was about to sigh with relief when the screaming started. Jeff didn't think, just hit the accelerator and got the hell out of there, but not before he saw a large woman running to something crumpled and still in the road not ten feet from the stuffed bear.

Jesus, I hit a kid... oh man

He pounded on the wheel.

Gotta go back

With an open beer in the van? Right, good one, genius.

Even if he got rid of the beer, they might determine he had had some, and then where would he be? And by leaving, wasn't it already a hit and run?

Hit and run – that's like manslaughter, right? Prison time, for sure.

He tried to convince himself that the second thing he had seen in the road was just a doll, but adults don't run into the street screaming and crying over a doll.

He wanted to go back. He wanted to go back and find the kid okay. Or maybe just scratched up a little... He could offer to give the kid and his mother a ride to the doctor. The mother would confide that she hadn't been paying attention and that she was lucky someone like him was there. They'd end up being friends and the kid would one day work for him.

Jeff realized he was going into some kind of shock, his mind spinning out impossibly positive scenarios followed by terrible and dire ones.

He kept making turns to make sure he wasn't followed by some mob group of vigilantes, who in his fevered mind were equipped with baseball bats, knives and hatchets.

He parked in an empty lot behind a dry cleaner, and got out to examine the front of his van. He nearly collapsed when his feet hit the pavement, as if his legs had gone asleep. Jeff grabbed the door and steadied himself, looking like a stereotypical drunk on a bender.

The front of the van was undamaged and unmarked. For one moment he told himself it didn't happen, then a small round object dropped from the bumper and rolled to his feet.

It was a tiny brass button, incised with the words "Oshkosh B'Gosh".

He vomited then, beer and his Sausage Egg McMuffin breakfast pouring from his mouth and spattering the lot of Speedee Cleaners.

He guessed others would have turned themselves in at that point. They'd do their time with dignity and grace, and devote themselves to good works, talking at schools and community centers about drinking and unsafe driving. Eventually they would find some measure of peace and become a beloved member of the community.

Not him. The thought of being locked in a prison cell made him feel ill. He hated being closed in, trapped like an animal. It was one of the reasons he had never sought out one of those cubicle jobs others seemed just fine with.

He wiped off the brass button with his shirt and tossed it down a storm drain.

Jeff took a circuitous route back to his apartment complex. He called his sister and said he had come down with a bug. She didn't believe him, but just figured he was too depressed to make the trip. He promised to mail his gifts and hung up, then unplugged the phone. He drank a six pack of Rolling Rock and passed out.

In his dreams the whole, terrible event slowed down like movie, moving just a few frames per second and allowing him to see what had only registered subliminally while he searched for a better song on the freakin' radio.

A little boy, dark with black hair, runs out into the street with his brown and orange teddy bear. He is dressed in green overalls with a yellow shirt. As the van bears down on him, he holds up his new bear.

Not in fear, but for Jeff to admire.

Then a gentle bump and he is gone.

A smile – the bear – he is gone.

Jeff woke up at three p.m., his mouth sour and lips caked with gummy saliva. He washed out his mouth with water, sucked some toothpaste out of the tube and swished it around with his tongue to get rid of the remaining sour sleep and puke taste.

He started to wash his face and inhaled a sour smell from the dirty washcloth.

He threw up in the toilet until he was wracked with dry heaves, the muscles in his abdomen cramping and releasing, leaving him as sore as if he had done dozens of sit ups.

Jeff cried then, leaning against the toilet, the earlier surges of adrenaline making the tragedy that had become his life now seem bleak and hopeless in the calm silence of his small apartment. He cried and cried, great jagged sobs purging him of every tear and, for a moment, all grief.

He went into the kitchen, more out of habit than hunger. The fridge only held two slices of cold pepperoni pizza and a squeeze bottle of ketchup. In the cupboard were boxes of Kraft Macaroni and Cheese and Hamburger Helper.

Screw it, he wasn't hungry any way. He tried to put a box of mac 'n' cheese away and misjudged where the shelf was. The box was knocked out of his hand and landed on the floor.

Jeff got mad.

Why the hell had that woman let her kid out into the street? He knew that area. Lots of people drove much more recklessly than he did, speeding at all hours, turning without signaling, backing out of driveways while talking on cell phones.

And if the kid, the smiling little bastard with his too-cute overalls and new bear, if he died?

What? What was he supposed to do?

He had been a tiny kid, for God's sake – it's not like he had dreams and plans and an engagement or a scholarship or job offer.

Jeff, on the other hand, was on the verge of a new life. He could make a difference in the world. He was a hard worker, and was good at making people laugh.

If the kid was dead, what good would it be for Jeff to get punished? Shouldn't the mother be punished? The street was a place for cars and trucks, not for tiny children in overalls.

He wanted to smash things, but was afraid of drawing attention to himself. Perhaps even now the cops were combing the neighborhood, looking for his van and just missing it in the parking garage out back… Until a 911 call about a man breaking windows in a rage brings them running…

He knew how it went, he watched television.

There's always some mistake made, and they close in and you're done. Gone is your dream of a new business and a new home and a new girl.

Gone is your new life.

Babies are the only ones with new life.

The phrase came to his mind unbidden. He tried to think

about what he would do next, but it became a mantra in his head, an annoying song trapped in an endless loop.

Babies are the only ones with new life.

Babies are the only ones with new life.

Babies are the only ones with new life.

He swept the coffee-maker off the counter, and the carafe shattered against the wall, spattering the surface with coffee and grounds.

Like old blood and brain matter.

He wondered if that was what was in the street right now, and puked up bitter yellow bile into the sink. He kept heaving, and his guts felt like they were being torn into ragged shreds. He hung onto the counter weakly, his legs nearly giving out, like a man at sea in a flimsy boat.

Jeff staggered to the couch and tried to drown out visions of green overalls and brightly colored bears with whatever the TV could conjure up.

He spent the night like that, his thoughts constantly replaying the accident and its outcomes. At five a.m. he dropped into an exhausted sleep, the TV filled with images of people meeting on party lines and college girls baring their breasts for $9.95.

His sleep was filled with images of college coeds holding up teddy bears or baring their breasts, only to suckle battered and bloody children.

He woke about seven and ate the pizza. His stomach lurched, but it stayed down. Jeff paced, considering his options. Part of him wanted to believe he could simply go on, that no one had gotten his license and that he was free and clear.

Losers in cop shows always feel that way, just before they're cuffed or brought down in a hail of bullets.

He had to leave.

It was the only way. People who stayed got caught.

He packed everything he could into an old duffel. He had a lot of books, mostly used paperbacks. Jeff loved to read, everything from science fiction to espionage and police procedurals. A lot of the classics, too. Dumas and Salinger, Dickens and Hemingway. Friends used to tell him he should go back to college, maybe teach English, but he hated the idea – it would almost be as bad as being cooped up in a cubicle all day. Nah, he'd stick with his landscaping plans. If he became a playwright, he could always work in the park or Starbucks, no need being trapped in a home or office.

He went through the books, and decided to take just a couple of old sci-fi books that he liked as a kid. The landlord could trash the rest or sell them.

Down in the parking garage he siphoned gas from the van into a galvanized bucket. He drove downtown, the gas sloshing over onto the floor of the van, the odor making him feel nauseous.

He didn't turn on the radio.

In the parking lot of Cresker Tool & Die, he put his duffel over near a light pole and then poured the remaining gasoline over the seats, dash and the worn carpeting in the foot wells. Jeff lit a book of matches and tossed them in, and the carpet blossomed into bright blue flames. He hurried off and collected his duffel, then waited in the shadows, hoping no one would come running with a fire extinguisher.

When the vehicle was an inferno he hurried away, trying to look casual and continually looking around like a fugitive. He was about a block away when he heard the soft *whumph* of the exploding gas tank, so like the sound of a small child being struck with a van.

The Greyhound Station came into view, and he never heard any sirens. He guessed fires downtown didn't warrant the attention they did in more upscale places like Santa Monica, where such disasters got prompt attention.

Jeff washed the gas smell off his hands in the restroom, using that crappy pink powder soap that always leaves your hands feeling gritty and soapy.

His hands still smelled like gas.

He wasn't hungry, but made himself eat a hot dog and drink a Sprite. The mustard smell proved more powerful than that of the gasoline, so he took several packets to the restroom and covered his hands with mustard, then washed them with pink soap, his hands looking like a child's balloons before becoming covered with foam.

The young guy at the ticket counter hardly gave him a glance. Jeff bought a ticket to Vegas and waited with the others, wondering if anyone else here had killed someone lately.

Unable to stop himself, he went to the little newsstand and bought a paper. A tiny gray box directed him to the story he had helped create.

TODDLER KILLED IN HIT AND RUN.

Jeff glanced around, certain he would meet the eyes of

some plainclothes detective who had been following him since the accident, perhaps even before.

People waited for their buses, most in a lackluster stupor. One couple was making out at the end of the row, and a high school kid was texting.

A mother nursing.

A kid reading a Kindle.

A homeless guy sleeping.

Some tourists sharing the photos on their phones and digital cameras.

The kid reading glanced his way, and then buried his nose back in his story.

No one gave a shit about him.

No one was following him.

He thought maybe he saw him, then, just a shimmer near the restroom doors, a movement out of the corner of his eye that he quickly dismissed as an optical illusion brought on by stress, fatigue and lack of nourishment.

The trip to Vegas was uneventful, the desert uncaring and bleak in the moonlight.

He paid cash for a motel on the outskirts of the strip, and waited for a couple of days to see if anyone would come forward.

No one did.

That is, not in the way he thought.

He found a job as a busboy at one of the casino coffee shops. It paid enough that soon he'd be able to get a cheap apartment, and he figured he would eventually start a pool or landscape business. There were a lot of high rollers living in the area who needed to keep their desert homes lush and verdant.

The sun was rising when Jeff returned to his motel from his first day on the job. The place was open twenty-four hours, and he had drawn the graveyard shift. He had winced when the manager told him that's what he had available, Jeff's mind filling with images of tiny clockwork coffins opening to let Kewpie doll mummies hold aloft their prized and bloodstained bears.

The motel was called The Firebird and rooms were discounted because the pool was being resurfaced. There was also a problem with the ice machine the clerk had informed him, a thin woman with bony arms clanking with dozens of bracelets.

He went to his room, a second floor piece of crap that looked out over the empty pool. Jeff drew the curtains, switched the air conditioning onto high and dropped onto the bed.

It had been a week and no one had come pounding on his door, surrounding the place with sharpshooters and squad cars, eventually leading him away in handcuffs while reporters labeled him a monster and a murderer.

A child killer.

He woke suddenly, the room pleasantly cool, and had to remind himself where he was.

He sensed motion in his peripheral vision, and a sort of shimmering light, as if he had left the TV on. Jeff turned, realizing as he did that the TV was on the other side of the room.

Before him, translucent and smiling, the little boy held up his bear.

Jeff recoiled, actually falling off the far side of the bed.

He panicked as he tried to extricate himself from the sheets and paper-thin blanket.

Jeff was sure the kid would appear where he was, perhaps to show a mouth filled with razor-sharp teeth and eyes black like a spider's.

No one appeared, and the room was silent except for the soft whirring of the air conditioner.

Jeff peeked over the bed, already convincing himself it was a dream.

The kid was there. He saw Jeff and smiled, raising the bear.

The child looked like he was made of light and spiderweb, some kind of impossible construction seen in CGI fantasies.

For a moment, Jeff convinced himself that some old friends were pranking him, that they had gotten together with some hologram expert to make him look like an asshole. But he knew that was just wishful thinking.

Forcing himself, Jeff reached out to touch the apparition. In TV shows with ghosts they always disappeared if you touched them. He figured it was worth a shot, but was trembling as he reached for one small shoulder.

He noticed a button missing on the overalls, and for a moment wondered how clothing also became... what was the word?

Ectoplasm.

He thought of all the ghost stories he had read as his hand

made its slow transit toward the boy. In those stories the incorporeal spirit is always cold. Jeff didn't register any drop in temperature, but as he tried to touch the child he encountered such a feeling of wrongness that he withdrew his hand, and clasped it protectively with the other. It had been like the feeling you get running into cobwebs in darkness, a panicked sensation not so much at what has happened, but what is to come.

It couldn't be a hologram – maybe it was just a hallucination.

Jeff closed his eyes tightly and counted to twenty – then fifty – then a hundred.

Still there.

Jeff whispered for him to leave.

He begged, he prayed, he threatened, though not too loudly. He still entertained the dread that the cops were even now triangulating his position from him using a nearby ATM.

No change.

Smile, bear.

Jeff turned on all the lights, opened the drapes, hoping to disperse the gossamer construction in a blast of Nevada sun.

It made him harder to see, but he was there.

Smile, bear.

Jeff left the motel, venturing out into the July heat, his body already wet with perspiration.

Wherever Jeff went, the child would reappear after fifteen minutes or so.

Inside a casino.

A movie theater.

A strip club.

Wal-Mart.

No one else saw him. No one else received that wide, innocent smile, that offering to share a precious toy.

Work became impossible. Even though he would turn his back on him – the boy never moved from whatever position he would appear in – but Jeff would know he was there. He once tried out-staring him, but he just regarded Jeff with those large eyes now all quicksilver and lacewing, seemingly ready to hold up the bear until the end of time.

Jeff found books on exorcism, but each ritual and invocation, every drop of holy water and waft of incense was met with good cheer and the silent invitation to regard the bear.

Jeff hired a medium, a ghost hunter, a *bruja* and a shaman from a local tribe.

The medium told him he was seeing the child spirit of his father. He sent her packing.

The ghost hunter told him his meters were detecting ten separate entities. Jeff kicked him out and put a "stop payment" on the check.

The shaman sensed the child, then seemed to listen to something. He smiled and told Jeff things were as they should be and left without payment.

The *bruja* spent the longest in the room. She looked right where the child was and regarded him silently for almost an hour.

At the end she told Jeff he should go back to Los Angeles and turn himself in so the child could rest.

Jeff had never told her where he was from, never showed her his driver's license or birth certificate.

The *bruja* left with her money, returning the child's smile and frowning at Jeff.

Turn himself in?

Bullshit.

He took a train from Nevada to Wyoming the next day. He left the child and bear at the station. Let the little bastard try and find him.

Jeff was stocking the drink case at a gas station in Jackson Hole ten days later when the child showed up. Jeff glanced up, saw him through the glass and dropped two sixes of bottled Budweiser. The boss docked him and Jeff knew he couldn't stay.

Jeff took a bus to Texas.

The kid rejoined him two weeks later.

Hitched to Florida.

Jeff awoke in the tub of a cheap motel to find the kid smiling at him.

Maine.

Iowa.

Georgia.

Oregon.

New York.

New Mexico.

Vancouver.

Jeff took every dime he had saved and bought a ticket to Maui. He found a job in a convenience store in the small town of Paia, serving burritos and corn dogs to surfers and local kids.

It took the child three months, but he found him.

# #

Jeff doesn't go out much, now. It's too hard for him to work with that kid staring, ever smiling, never accusing. Holding up that bear for him.

His image is clearest at Christmas, then it slowly fades like a waning moon over the months to June, then waxes again.

As constant and ever-present as the moon.

The ghost child smiles, holds up his bear.

It's not like a film clip that runs on a loop – there are subtle differences each time – and Jeff knows the child sees him, though he cannot explain it any more than one can explain how you know a person or an animal sees you even if there is no other communication. There is something in the eyes that registers you, regards you.

Judges you?

Jeff lives off canned food and TV, seeing the little boy continually out of the corner of his eye, always cheerful, always full of life.

Jeff will wait. The kid will get tired and leave him.

And then Jeff can begin his new life.

SPOOKED

I will warn that this is not a pretty story, nor does it end happily.

Perhaps I should amend that, as it does end happily for some, but not for me or me mate, and I reckon I am a bit biased when the outcome does not favor us.

The three of us (aye, there was a third and that is the root of our troubles) grew up on the streets of London. It's not that we were orphans or had a lack of loving parents, it's just everyone was poor in them days, and it was hard not to notice certain ladies and gentlemen in finery what had it better than you, and maybe you and your mates wanted to do something about it. Even the odds, you might say. And, if you were able to nick a purse and buy yourself a bit of candy, and then maybe come home with a joint to roast or some fresh eggs bought with what was left over, and your mum wanted to know what you was up to, then maybe you could put on your most innocent face, and say what that you had done an errand or two for a few bob.

Oh, and then you were the hero of the family, weren't you?

Even your old dad was impressed with your entrepreneurial spirit. But it wouldn't do too often; such lies become weighty and cumbersome, overstuffed birds that can't fly.

Now that I am grown, I realize that my parents probably knew such fortune was ill-gotten and based on the lifting of pocket watches and pinching of purses, and yet they had mouths to feed, mouths without my talents or questionable ethics. So nothing was said except that I was a "fine lad" and that I made them proud.

So, I don't think it's too large a leap to say my parents encouraged my life of crime, do you? Oh, I'm not saying I lay all my ills at their feet, God rest them, but if they didn't set me on this road then they certainly didn't discourage me, neither.

I realize the night is cold and your time is short, so I will jump ahead a few years.

So it was always us three: Tom Morris, Bob Thackeray and me, Charlie Addison. Me and Tom were both tall and lean, him being a bit taller, while Bob was stout with a ruddy face and a shock of red hair, continually in disarray.

Bob was no good at running, but he was quite an expert on crying and spinning yarns, terrible little tales about mothers selling their virtue and little sisters gone blind from working with lye in a soap plant. He would cry then, honest to goodness tears, as his face turned as red as a beet. If the gentleman or lady gave him a few pence, we let them be, but if their hearts remained stony and their purses closed, then Tom and I would make sure their charitable donations were especially large.

This served us as boys, but young men cannot cry for mum and little sis without rousing suspicions. By now, we had all become independent of our troubled parents and thus were free to attempt more daring snatches, with Bob (now of truly prodigious girth) stepping into the path of our pursuers at the most opportune (for us) moment and creating a fleshy wall they could not easily surmount as we made our escape.

This was a fine enterprise for a couple of years, and we were careful not to be too greedy lest our faces and practices become known to the local constabulary. A bar man at a pub we favored told us suspicions were being levied against friend Bob, so we decided it was time to enter a new phase of our criminal pursuits.

Around that time, medical colleges were in short supply of bodies for study. A whole generation of young doctors needed corpses to practice their art upon, and these were much too scarce to insure each future man of medicine could get plenty of experience cutting and sewing and whatnot. The three of us had seen dead bodies on several occasions, a kid we knew who drowned in the Thames, an old man who collapsed in the street, a hard man stabbed in a pub row. So, while the work might seem grisly, we were prepared for its gruesome nature and looked forward to receiving recompense while advancing the medical sciences.

We were sure our late mums would be proud.

Here I must digress and tell you a bit more about the three of us mates, urchins united in boyhood, would-be master criminals and advancers of science in adulthood.

Tom was me best mate, and a truer friend I would never expect to see in this lifetime or the next. We had gotten each other out of dozens of scrapes, never ratted on one another, even when the coppers was acting like the other had sold us out to trick a confession out of us – I tend to think them Blue Bottles what have the badges and billies are as dishonest in their own ways as we are in ours. And Tom and me, we always had each other's back when dealing with the fairer sex. If Tom told some curly-topped miss he was employed by Her Majesty in some adventurous (and legitimate) endeavor, I would always lend credible support and enthusiastic corroboration to his tale, as he would do for me.

Bob, now, was a different matter all together.

As I said, we had known him since boyhood and liked him well enough, but noticed a peculiar evolution as he got older and fatter.

He became more and more talkative, and more and more boring.

It wasn't that he was some glock, a halfwit like my cousin Teddy who got kicked in the head by a draft horse and was never quite right, always drooling and singing nonsense.

Bob was in his right mind, just bleeding boring.

Boring? Take the most boring person, story or bit of drivel you know, and multiply by one hundred.

Bob would go on for hours and hours about the most mundane and wretched topics, such as how to properly pickle an eel, which baker had the best bread or what the possibility of a storm would be by week's end.

Me and Tom weren't sure how this came about. We suspected his parents, whom we had only known by their glares and fixed stares as boys, were also relentlessly dull and this trait had slowly blossomed in Bob like a loathsome and odious flower.

It got so he was a right pox with women, sending them

running before either Tom or I could tell them about tea with Her Majesty. And the cute little boy who could open hearts and wallets with tales of misspent childhoods and ailing mums now only made people check their watches and cough their excuses before running out in search of something other than the hideously dull conversements of one Robert Christian Thackeray of Pick Street.

In ordinary friendships you can tell an unwanted bloke to find another pub and that's that. With some, a bloodied nose and a few loosened teeth create the proper motivation to seek libation elsewhere.

But when you have been career criminals with someone, when the list of your sins and offenses stretches back through the years like a road to ruin, it is not so easy to disentangle one's self from a boring and talkative colleague. You cannot lose them or run them off because there is always a danger they will turn on you, hurt feelings creating ripe conditions through which betrayal and confession seem like the cure-all for their woes.

Much as I hate prison, the thought of being also cooped up with Bob Thackeray every bleeding day and night made me feel like I might have to kill myself.

I know you're thinking to yourself that murder might solve all our problems in regards to Bob Thackeray, but neither Tom or I was a killing type. Strictly larceny and burglary, if you please. We weren't the types to set fires or endanger folks, kidnap heiresses or get involved in acts of anarchy.

So, our solution was to do a job, have one drink with Bob and then make excuses of little women who needed us at home. Although Tom and I saw a number of girls, there was none we had tripped down the aisle with, and none who demanded the majority and quality of our post-job time. However, Bob did not know that. When he hinted as to how he might like to pop round for supper and a pint, we fabricated shrewish witches who wanted us all to themselves, leaving our "worthless mates" in the "back alleys, trash heaps and coal bins where they belonged." Then we'd congratulate old Bob on being wise enough to remain a bachelor, bid adieu, then nip off to the Four Piglets or the Fox and Fife for wine, women and Bob-less song.

You might feel you know what's coming, and I assure you do not. I was there and I didn't, nor did Tom, who's better at ciphers and figures than me.

So, we were making a few quid by digging up fresh corpses and taking them to the medical college. Now, of course, everyone knew of the dealings of Burke and Hare some twenty years before in Scotland, but Tom, Bob and I pledged never to resort to murder to fulfill our quota. It seemed there was always plenty of fresh grist for the medical mill, if you will excuse my colorful turn of phrase.

Usually Tom and me did the digging, and Bob ran interference with any caretakers or constables who happened along. Once again his weeping skills were brought to bear as he essayed portrayals of bereaved husbands, uncles, fathers and brothers. Will Shakespeare at his most eloquent could not have elicited more tears from hardened coppers or watchmen as did old Bob.

Now, we were always careful to cover up the evidence of our nocturnal shopping trips, so no one would suspect that any of our recent visits had resulted in the plucking of graveyard fruit from its earthen basket. And thus, my friends, no alarums and excursions against grave robbers had occurred in our little quarter of London.

Still, one makes assumptions and these are the devil's snares. We thought we were safe because we were patient and careful.

I must sadly confess now that this was not the case.

Our target for that night's work was a young bride who had died from a nasty fall on a slippery cobbled street. It was coming on autumn and the bloody English rain made something of a misery of our work, but it also led to happy accidents like this one. Doctor Earle at the college paid a bonus for young women of childbearing age, as there were mysteries in such creatures that neither I (nor doctors, apparently) had parsed out.

It's a sad thing to find such a lovely flower buried so deep, but we needed the funds.

I should mention here that we often relieved the corpses of their worldly jewelry and watches if they had any. The doctors would not pay us for such finery and you certainly weren't going to see someone on a doctor's slab with watch and fob. It may seem strange to you, but this was a greater crime than removing the body from its loamy bed. Such is the world we live in.

The young woman in question, one Agnes Moorehouse, had a lovely pearl necklace that would easily fetch us a quid with a fence with whom Tom and I were acquainted.

Now, unknown to us, the widower Moorehouse, Agnes's husband Clancy, was a greedy git. He, with no criminal record whatsoever, had suddenly decided he didn't like such a valuable piece of jewelry staying with his missus as she turned from flesh to bone to dust. Old Clancy had plans for the money he could get, he did.

So, while Tom and I were performing a delicate "pearl-ectomy" from the lovely and cold neck of his missus, Clancy was creeping up with a pick and shovel.

Old Bob, ever loyal, popped up to waylay young Clancy, unaware he was armed with a farm implements. He buried the pick in the soft earth of Bob's head, and I am afraid I must report to you that both Tom and I ran from the graveyard, our clothes spattered with bits of our old friend.

Of course, this would be a sad ending for any tale, and you might think that next I would inform you that Tom and I saw the error of our ways and now did good works at orphanages and hospitals, all in the name of our friend Bob Thackeray.

Were it the truth, I might still be a happy man.

In fact, the killing of old Bob got Clancy in some hot water, as old Bob was recognized by the caretaker as a frequent mourner, and Clancy had to explain to the constable just what he was doing in a graveyard with pick and shovel. Our work unearthing his missus just helped seal his fate, as it were.

Tom and I were questioned, but had ready alibis at the Four Piglets, where the barman and three patrons swore we had been in an impromptu darts tournament at the hour said grave was being defiled.

One happy note, Tom and me were able to deduct the pearls from this awful equation, and used the proceeds to have a rambunctious, if somewhat exclusive, wake for old Bob.

At said wake, me and Tom decided we were through with grave robbing. Winter would be coming on and we both thought the idea of digging in frozen, snow-covered earth was not work suitable for men of our talents. We had enough to lay low until spring, and then we might turn to some confidence game what to relieve wealthy citizens of their worldly goods and bank notes.

It's nice to dream, isn't it?

It was nearly Christmas when we had to admit to ourselves that we weren't very good confidence men, nor were we likely to be. Any confidence game requires a bit of play-acting, a lot of confidence (swagger) and some sleight of hand that goes beyond mere games of "chance" for cocky squires just off the boat.

Tom and me didn't have none of those things, in spades. We were contemplating going back to grave robbing in the spring, and wondering who might take old Bob's place.

That's when old Bob sat down at our table and said, "Hallo, gents."

As you might have guessed, our dear departed mate was now a ghost, albeit a large one. He looked the same as, well, like he did before some of his features were rearranged by a pickax, only now he looked like he was woven out of gossamer and moonlight. I know that sounds sort of lovely and poetic, but Bob was an ugly bloke, ghost or no.

Tom dropped his glass and the barman shouted that he would have to pay for it.

I looked at him. "You see him, too."

He nodded, and said, "Old Bob."

"Now then," Bob said, "don't talk about me like I'm not here, because I am."

We both mumbled apologies, Tom and me, wondering if we'd gone crackers.

"You're not crazy," Bob said, as if reading our thoughts, "it's me. I am a spirit." He said that last with a bit of a flourish, as if he were rather proud of it.

"So you did die," said Tom.

Bob looked at him somewhat patronizingly, which I believe was a first.

"Why aren't you in Heaven, then, or... Or the other place?" Tom demanded.

"For your information," said Bob, "I saw Heaven, very lovely with golden towers and plenty of food and ale and chocolates by the handful... And the girl angels are the prettiest girls you have ever laid eyes on."

"So then, why are you here bothering us?" Tom asked sourly.

"You're my mates - I couldn't leave you behind."

At this point, it came to my attention that no one in the pub was paying old Bob any mind. You'd think a ghost might attract a bit of attention, even amongst a crowd as pickled as them what patronized the Four Piglets.

"Bob," I said, "how come no one else has taken a notice of you?"

Bob beamed. "I can show myself to a select group, or stay invisible - it's one of the first things you learn."

An idea was forming in my brain, then. But I was foggy from ale and my first encounter with the supernatural, and I wanted nothing more than to sleep.

"Bob, my friend, it has been great, this little impromptu

reunion, but I am in some serious need of sleep."

Tom murmured his agreement.

"But I only just got here!" Bob wailed, and several patrons looked up, each visibly pale.

"Look," I hissed, "you may be a specter what only requires a cat nap in a belfry now and then, but us flesh and blood types need rest."

Bob nodded glumly.

A thought occurred to me, of all the times we had lied to Bob about being married and a required presence in our homes with our wives. Such a falsehood had gotten us away from corporeal Bob, and I had a feeling ectoplasmic Bob wasn't much better.

"Bob, you wouldn't... you wouldn't peek in on Tom or me uninvited, would you?"

Bob looked horrified. "I would never disturb your privacy - you're me mates!"

I nodded, satisfied. "Well, we'd love to chat further, but both Tom and me have to carry on with our husbandly duties. You understand, don't you, Bob?"

Bob nodded miserably. "I suppose I could go practice scaring drunken sots down by the docks."

I patted him on the shoulder, but my hand went right through. "That sounds like a right capital idea, Bob - practice makes perfect, doesn't it?"

Outside the Four Piglets, we watched our friend float away, head down.

"I feel a bit bad lying to him," I said.

Tom waved me off. "He's dead, Charlie. If he can get over that, he can get over anything."

I went home, but I didn't go to sleep. I kept thinking what we might accomplish with an actual ghost as part of our enterprise. I remembered reading about con games where fake mediums and other charlatans pretended to have contact with the dead. We'd have them all beat, because our ghost would be real!

The next day, Tom and I met down by the docks at our usual spot. As we figured, Bob joined us, as always. He was a little more difficult to see in the daytime, but we could hear him plain, and there was a sort of "heat shimmer" that he called his "manifestation."

I told Bob and Tom about my idea for using Bob's status as a phantom to dip deep into the pockets and purses of the wealthy bereaved.

I looked at Bob. "First things, first. Can you contact the recently departed?"

"Only if they haven't crossed over," he said. "Once they do - in either direction - they are out of range of both the living and the not-so-living like me."

I thought a moment. That limited us, some. Unless...

"Can you alter your looks, Bob?"

"What?"

"Say a rich couple lost their little boy - could you take on his appearance?"

Bob sounded doubtful. "I... I dunno. They didn't teach us

anything like that. We did get some lessons in looking scary, but not disguising ourselves."

"That's no good, anyway," Tom said, "he wouldn't sound like the little urchin, would he? He wouldn't sound like anyone but himself."

"He doesn't need to sound like them, my argumentative friend - he'd be speaking through one of us, the medium."

Some clouds scudded across the sky and Bob was easier to see. He was still wearing the suit he was buried in, which had been one of his favorites. I wondered how a suit of clothes could become ghostly.

Then Bob waved at something or someone we couldn't see.

Tom looked at me. "No one, and I mean no one, is going to buy a bloke as a medium. It's always some old woman, preferably made up like a gypsy with scarves and what-not."

"So we enlist the services of some old auntie." I said, and then turned to Bob. "Who were you waving at, just now?"

"Oh, that was old man MacTavish, who used to live on High Street."

"MacTavish, the fellow what owns the Bristol Fishing Line?"

"Yeah. Just died. Heart attack, I think."

I looked at Tom. "I think our fortunes have just turned, my lads."

"You gonna hold a séance for old man MacTavish?" Tom asked.

"No, something better. Let us adjourn to the Fox and Fife

to slake our thirsts."

My plan was deceptively simple and, I thought, fiendishly clever. Part of the great risk of burgling houses is getting caught. You may case a joint from now until doomsday, but you are never sure on the night in question when a Blue Bottle might be making the rounds, ready to alert his copper friends, or what the complement might be of dogs, servants, out of town guests and other random factors what can result in incarceration or worse.

We had the perfect scout, one that couldn't be seen or killed. What's more, he could alert us when someone of prominence had died, and we could swoop in and get all the best stuff before the lawyers and greedy relatives could get their hands on it.

It seemed foolproof.

We started with old man MacTavish. Bob alerted us after he had searched the house from top to bottom. MacTavish didn't have much of a staff, only a woman to come in a clean and cook for him, and she went home after dinner. Happily for us, MacTavish had had his heart attack on her day off. He didn't own a dog and no one guarded his premises.

What's more, Bob had found a rather attractive wall safe behind a painting of the Golden Hind. None of us was accomplished safe crackers (and Bob, being a ghost, couldn't move the dial), but Tom was pretty sure we could knock off the door of the safe with some chisels and a stout sledge hammer.

I am pleased to say the house was a right deadlurk, empty as a church on Monday, and the burglary went off very well, netting us a tidy sum in gold, silver and a couple of right nice watches. We were unable to crack the safe, but decided it probably just held papers, a will and other things we would be unable to convert to cash.

It wasn't anything like the king's ransom we had all been secretly hoping for, but was enough that we could afford to lay low a while and choose our next target carefully.

Bob watched sadly as we split the proceeds 50/50. He had no heirs, no family, no favorite auntie living in seclusion. It was just old Bob, and a ghost has no use for pound notes.

Tom thumbed his stack of bills and said, "What do you say to a few rounds at the Four Piglets, lads, first pint's on me."

"Yar, and the first dollymop," I said, leering. It was an old joke but we laughed.

Except Old Bob.

"You're going to the pub... now?" he asked.

"Sure we are - that's where the ale is… and the girls."

Bob just nodded sadly.

"Come on, Bob, you know you are invited, don't you?"

He nodded, his frown curving down even more.

"Aw, don't be like that," Tom said, "don't you want to join us?"

"Can't drink," pouted Bob. "Can't even smell it or feel the foam on me nose. I used to love that."

"Well, then, what about girls? You must have met a few spooks in skirts in the last few weeks," I said.

"Sure, they're pulling dollymops out of the Thames almost every bloody day," Tom said cheerfully. "Surely one of them's caught your fancy."

"They call me a right git and tell me to go hang myself," admitted Bob sadly. "It's not like when I'm with you lot, and there's plenty of skirts to go 'round."

This was true. And if we was flush, usually there'd be one miss or two too drunk to discern that Bob's conversational skills were roughly those of a dead mackerel.

I looked at Tom while Bob glumly eyed a cockroach making his way across the floor.

"You're kidding me, right?" Tom asked.

"He netted us the biggest score of our lives and can't even take a cut. We owe him, Tom."

Tom sighed. "I hate when you turn ethical, Mr. Addison."

I looked at Bob, whose head had disappeared into the wall, presumably following the cockroach.

"Bob, why don't you come along and we'll see if there isn't a spectral girl waiting for you at the pub.

Bob nearly danced all the way there, he was so happy.

There was a girl there, a ladybird named Phyllis all of us had known. Luckily, she had been murdered in White Chapel just two nights earlier. Luckier still, she knew Bob and enjoyed his company the last time we had all celebrated in the flesh.

She was happy for the company, but now she was incapable of getting drunk. And Bob, bless him, was hard pressed to find interesting topics, since anything of a criminal nature was off limits. This is a hard lesson we had learned from seeing some of our colleagues wearing the broad arrow, which is to say they were guests of the local prison. Their downfall had come at the hands of some ladybird who just had to sing.

So Bob went on and on about things he missed, the cockroach he had followed, and different bird calls he thought he could do with some accuracy.

I have to say, someone who is accomplished at bird calls is insufferable in under five minutes… And, if they are like Bob and truly horrible at it, well, one call is more than enough.

To make matters worse, we could not get any of our own girls, because we were carrying on a four-way conversation where two of the participants seemed to be nonexistent, giving one the fairly accurate impression that Tom and I were crackers.

Phyllis finally left in disgust, and nothing Tom or I could say would dissuade her.

Tom and me endured another two hours of blather about cockroaches, the pickling of eels and birds of northern Britain before begging off to go home to our nonexistent and shrewish wives.

The next job was about month later, on Stir-up Sunday. While everyone else was attending church or eating their puddings, we were happily helping ourselves to the worldly goods of the Widow Parkhurst, who, while not being fabulously wealthy, had a habit of stuffing biscuit tins full of pound notes. By the time we had gotten under every loose floorboard and behind every mortar-less fireplace brick, Tom and me had netted something like a hundred pounds. We could live like kings if we were careful, but probably better to live like dukes and not raise suspicions.

"What we need," said Tom, "is one grand caper what

provides for us for the rest of our lives, living like royalty in France or Spain."

"Yeah, quite a standard of living you'll have," I said, "you being ignorant in French, Spanish and a host of other foreign tongues."

Tom said coolly, "I shall become rich enough to learn, and some delightful maiden of said country will tutor me on both her mother tongue and how one lives as the upper crust."

Bob, of course, was sad as we divided up the spoils. Now that his part of the caper was over, the only thing he had to look forward to was our company. Tom and I had already decided we couldn't stand another evening of bird calls and ghostly observations of the Old Bob sort.

When he mentioned the Four Piglets and gamely joked, "My treat," we had our excuses at the ready.

Tom said, "Love to, old boy, but the wife has been nipping at my heels about wallpapering the sitting room. Duty calls."

And I chimed in, "And me Margaret has been threatening to break some bottles over my head if I come home drunk."

"I don't think your wives love you very much," complained Bob, "after all, a man's home is his castle and all that."

"True enough, Mr. Thackeray, but I love her," I said, putting a hand over my heart for emphasis.

"And we're married, so that's that," Tom offered.

We left Bob and went to a pub called The Wolf's Tale that he didn't know about.

On Christmas Eve, Bob came to us fairly jumping with

excitement.

"I found it!" he exclaimed.

"Found what?" Tom countered.

"The last job you ever need do," Bob said, dancing a little hornpipe.

"Who died?" I asked.

"Lord Kensington-Smythe, the Duke of Suffolk," Bob offered.

"Are you daft?" Tom said, "His Lordship is always surrounded by staff and lackeys and such like."

"But not this time," Bob said. "He's got a hideaway for his trysts, and it's far from prying eyes."

"So he's got a hidey-hole in the woods," Tom grumbled, "What are we stealing, a vase of posies and some snuff?"

"What would you say to a thousand gold crowns?" Bob offered.

Tom and I stared at him, each of us trying to picture that much money.

"And why..." My throat was dry and I took a sip of ale. "Why would he have so much money in such a place?"

Bob grinned. "He's on her Majesty's business. Meeting some swell from France... Some sort of alliance thing."

"And you're sure about this?" Tom asked.

"Got it from his Lordship himself," Bob said.

"And why would he tell you?" I asked.

"Because he's sure that someone will steal it, so he is trusting me to tell her Majesty of his death and the missing gold."

"And he's already passed on?" I asked.

Bob nodded. "Saw him ascend the golden stair about two hours ago."

I clapped him on the back. "Lead the way, your Lordship."

The three of us laughed at that. I think it may be the last time I laughed.

The cottage was right where Bob said it was, and was dark. It was close to midnight, and Tom and I expected a very happy Christmas that year.

Bob floated on in. After a moment, his arm emerged from the door and waved us in – all clear. We picked the lock, and entered the dwelling. As we had with graves, we always tried to enter and leave without damaging property, as it gave the Blue Bottles less to go on.

Tom and I stepped inside, letting our eyes grow accustomed to the gloom.

"Hurry!" Bob said, raising his voice, startling both me and Tom.

He also startled Lord Jeremy Kensington-Smythe, Duke of Suffolk, who appeared in the doorway, very much alive and carrying a fowling piece.

His first shot took off most of Tom's head. I tripped over my late companion and that gave the Duke enough time to blast away a good portion of my chest and vitals...

# #

I remember a sort of gray fog, then waking up near The Four Piglets.

Tom and Bob were there, and Tom was as ghostly as Bob.

"So now there are two ghosts in the family," I joked.

"Better look in a mirror, mate," Tom replied.

The window of the pub was sufficient, and the reflection there was me, only one of ectoplasm and spider silk, not flesh, blood and bone.

I looked at Bob. "I thought you said the Duke was dead"

Bob looked down, ashamed.

"He lied," Tom said, "He actually told his Lordship that two 'assassins' would visit him before dawn on Christmas morning.

"Why would you do that?" I screamed at Bob.

"Because you and Tom are my mates, and your wives were making you miserable!" he countered, spectral tears running down his cheeks.

I looked at Tom and he looked at me. Hoisted on our own petards, as it were. I told you we were lousy con men.

It took a few days, but Bob was able to teach Tom and me the finer points of ghostdom. It was worse than he painted it, because you can't smell, touch or taste anything. Oh, you can see and hear plenty, but those senses are useless for enjoying a pint or a dollymop or a game of darts.

At the end of a week, Bob had driven us nearly insane with his usual drivel and constant apologizing and rationalizing. I whispered to Tom that I could hardly wait for Heaven, if it meant shedding this ghostly existence and losing Bob in the angelic multitudes.

Tom spat on his hand and we shook on it.

The very next day, a stair appeared in the middle of High Street. It wasn't golden, but slate, and it didn't go up, not an inch. It led down and down into a sulfurous pit with lots of screaming.

I didn't like it.

Tom looked at Bob. "Where's our golden stairway, then?"

Bob shrugged. "I've only seen it when someone of virtue ascends. For blokes like us, it's a choice of being ghosts or burning."

I looked at the pit, miles down and filled with the anguish of the Damned. I looked at Bob, picturing an eternity of his anecdotes and observations.

"What are you gonna do, Charlie?" Tom asked.

"I'm thinking," I said, "I'm thinking."

THE INNKEEPER'S TALE

Long ago, there were several good inns in the Black Forest, but none quite so well-known as The Red Lion.

Some said it was because the food, simple but hearty, tasted like nothing on Earth, and surely was enchanted somehow. The same case was made for the ale, which was supposedly brought in from a local monastery. But rumor had it that it was actually made by gnomes or dwarves far off in the uncharted reaches of pine and fir.

Some praised the music, some the beds, others the expert care of horses as well as guests.

Whether a traveler or local, all agreed that the proprietor, Helmut Zauberwald, was the most congenial of hosts, anxious to please and always fair in his dealings. Not only did his business flourish, but he was blessed with a beautiful and loving wife Gerta and a daughter Dorothea who was as fair as spring in the mountains.

Many wished to court Dorothea, but Helmut would simply tell them she was already promised. Dorothea, for her part, was a sweet and winsome girl. She would often entertain the guests by singing while accompanying herself on the lute. Those that heard her said no bird could sing any sweeter. To the flirtatious advances of travelers she would laugh and move deftly out of the way of their slaps and pinches. Good thing, for anyone pinching her would surely have been thrown into the Kalte Quelle River by her father, who had become strong as a youth carrying casks of ale and bags of flour, when his father had built the Red Lion with his grandfather.

One day in late December, a young man chanced upon The Red Lion. His name was Peter and he was bound for Munich to seek his fortune. A handsome lad, he also had a fine voice, and joined Dorothea in several of her songs.

Helmut saw a look pass between them and his heart grew heavy. In the kitchen he confided in Gerta, and she tried to put his fears to rest.

"Do not fret, husband, she is a good girl."

"But there is so much she doesn't know about the world, Gerta. Particularly the world beyond this forest."

"She knows enough not to go off with strangers, dear Helmut, now help me serve our guests."

Peter eliminated all of Helmut's worries about his designs on Dorothea when he said he would not be staying the night.

"But the day is half gone," protested Helmut, ever the good host, "you won't make many miles before nightfall."

"I promised an aunt I would spend Christmas day with them," Peter said. "They are only half a day's ride from here, so I will be there just after dark."

Helmut had Gerta pack the young man a hearty lunch. He saw sadness in Dorothea's eyes when the young man rode off, and decided he would be especially gentle with her this Christmas.

How trusting he was!

In truth, Peter doubled back late in the night, when everyone except Dorothea was asleep. It was a tribute to her way with all creatures that neither horse nickered as the couple approached, and soon they were far from The Red Lion.

At dawn the next morning, once her mother saw that the cow had not been milked nor the chickens fed, she rushed to Dorothea's room, a heavy feeling in her heart.

The girl's bed was neatly made, and a little note said simply,

Mama and Papa,

Do not be angry, I love him so. I will contact you when we reach Munich.

Your loving daughter, Dorothea.

She brought the note to Helmut, her eyes full of tears. Helmut wanted to curse the boy, but could not. He remembered what love was like at that age, all heat and light, without sense or wisdom.

"By now they will have left the forest," Gerta whispered, and began to weep anew.

Helmut told her to carry on with their guests, he would find their daughter.

"Take Jürgen the Huntsman and Gustav the Woodcutter

with you," she said.

"And have them know the secret we have been keeping?" he asked. "They might keep silent, but it would get out… I couldn't bear that."

"We should have told her, at least," said Gerta, wringing her hands.

Helmut kissed her tenderly and hitched their best horse to the wagon they took to town to fetch supplies. He knew the way to Munich, and prayed he would catch up to them before it was too late.

He found them six hours later, just outside the boundary of the Black Forest.

Peter saw him and ran to him, pale and frightened.

"Herr Zauberwald, I am so sorry – she took ill quite suddenly and couldn't ride… I thought it might be a fever but it's gotten so much worse…"

Helmut wanted to strike the boy, but Dorothea was his first concern.

She was under a tree, resting on a blanket, and his heart filled with a grievous ache when he saw her.

Dorothea's lustrous red hair had fallen out, and her skin had gone the color and texture of dead leaves.

A small moan escaped his lips and she opened her eyes. Those eyes, once so bright and green, were now a sickly yellow.

"Papa, what is wrong with me?" she gasped, though it sounded more like dried leaves skittering across a stone floor.

Helmut tried to lift her, but she was as light as an empty

chrysalis. If he tried to carry her or put her on a horse she would surely fall apart and be carried away on the wind.

Helmut looked at Peter. "There are two buckets in the wagon. Go into the forest and find a clear stream. Bring me back a bucket of water and a bucket of earth from beneath a moss-covered tree."

Peter wanted to protest, but a look at the old man told him this was no time for arguing.

While Peter went to fetch these things, Helmut stood vigil over his daughter.

Her skin was becoming gray, and bits of her flesh simply drifted off like ash.

"When your mother and I were young," Helmut told her, "we found we were unable to have children. At first, we thought that would be all right, because the inn would keep us busy and the village's children would be our surrogates."

He looked down at her, fighting the urge to caress her, to try and comfort her.

"But it wasn't enough," he went on. "We tried all the old remedies, the old wives' tales, but nothing worked." He stroked her cheek, his touch lighter than a butterfly. Tears fell from his eyes onto his beloved daughter, and her dry skin absorbed them.

Peter returned with the buckets of earth and water. Helmut motioned him forward and the boy came quietly. He gasped when he saw how frail and gray Dorothea had become.

Helmut motioned at him impatiently and Peter placed the buckets near him.

Helmut wet his hand and began to let water drip over the

face and body of his stricken daughter. She sighed as the water touched her.

"When you are an innkeeper," he continued, "you hear many stories, especially living near a forest like ours. I had heard tales of the *Lutzelfrau*, or Yule Witch, an old crone who lives in the woods. Some say she is just an old woman who collects roots and herbs. Others say she is a witch, and that she preys on the unwary and eats children. I didn't want to believe those stories, but packed a knife in my bedroll, just in case.

"Gerta and I rode deep into the forest, and passed through places I'd sooner not think about, let alone visit again. There are dark places there, darker than just being without light, where the eye catches only a glimpse, the ear only a whisper, but I can tell you I am fairly certain that trolls and gnomes and other such things do dwell there, and not all are friendly to men."

Helmut dripped the last of the water on Dorothea and was relieved to see her color going from gray to brown, and some patches of brown turning red, or yellow.

He began to take little bits of earth and sprinkle them on his daughter. Peter looked at him and Helmut nodded. Peter followed his example and began to sprinkle the rich dark earth on the girl.

"We found an old cottage near nightfall," Helmut continued, "and an old woman invited us in out of the cold. I had brought a ham and a keg of ale and offered it to her, and she was grateful. Over supper we told her of our woes, and she said she might help. Then she told us she was tired and needed her sleep. She asked me to check that her small barn was locked, because there were 'things' in the forest that wanted to steal her cow. I went out into the darkness with a small lantern, and heard things off beyond the trees making the most terrible sounds. Worse, I heard music that was so eerily beautiful that I wanted to go to it. Had Gerta not been along with me on that journey I would have gone, and I suspect I would never have returned to my home. As it was, it was a tremendous effort to check on the livestock, all the while trying to ignore the Sirens' call. My boots crunched along a path of the small white stones that ran from the cottage to the barn.

"The cow was in her stall and our horses were also secure inside. I was about to leave when my lantern saw something golden in the farthest stall. Curious, I went to look. There, in the hay, were sacks and sacks of gold coins. Even one would have made Gerta and I rich beyond our wildest dreams. We could have sold the inn and lived like royalty in Munich or Paris.

"But it wasn't mine to take. We had come to seek the old woman's help, and now I would rob her? I wouldn't do it. I didn't so much as touch the money, lest a coin find its way into my purse."

Dorothea's skin was now a yellow-green, but her breathing sounded more normal.

"I went back into the cottage," Helmut said, "and curled up on a pallet with Gerta. My sleep was deep and dreamless. In the morning, we found that the old woman, who called herself Hecate, had made a small doll of pine needles tied with red thread. She took a hair from each of us and wrapped it around the doll. She then burned the doll in a metal bowl while she chanted something. It was no language I had ever heard, but it reminded me of the singing I had heard the night before.

"When all that was left of the doll was a small bit of ash, she mixed this into two cups of tea and made us each drink. Then she told us to go home and 'let nature take its course.'"

The last of the earth had been spread on Dorothea and Peter was amazed to see it had been absorbed into her body. She was breathing stronger now, and when Helmut lifted her he was grateful to find that there was now substance to her.

He and Peter placed her in the wagon. Peter tied his horse to the back of the wagon and rode with Helmut.

"The Yule Witch gave us a warning," Helmut said, "she told us our daughter would be human in every way, but she would always be a child of the forest and could never leave it. We never needed to travel outside of its boundaries, so it was never a problem. We named her Dorothea because it means 'Gift from God,' and she has always been so to us."

Peter hung his head. "I am sorry I lied to you, Herr Zauberwald."

"I can see you love each other," said Helmut, "and I cannot fault you for that. Is life in Munich so important?"

"My heart knows only Dorothea," said Peter.

"If you can be content to work at the inn until you are wed, and make your living in the Black Forest, then I will give you my blessing."

Peter was so excited he could not speak, but his smile gladdened Helmut's heart.

When they entered the boundary of the Black Forest, they heard a rustling. Looking back in the wagon, Peter was shocked see Dorothea completely encased in a cocoon of bright, green leaves. As he watched, the leaves parted and a pale hand emerged.

By the time they reached the inn, Dorothea was well again, and hugged her father and mother when told they would bless her marriage to Peter.

They were married the next Christmas, and had four children, each born in the spring. All grew straight and tall, and all had a way with animals that some claimed was almost magical.

Peter lived to be a very old man of ninety-five. He died peacefully, attended by his wife, children and grandchildren. As for Dorothea, it is said she and her children live there still, protecting the Black Forest which gives them life.

HE'LL BE COMIN' DOWN THE CHIMNEY, DOWN

The house was old but solid, and the front door was secured with a padlock - a pretty new one, by the look of it. No problem. Johnny B check up and down the street for nosy neighbors and then vaulted the side fence that protected a weed-choked lawn and rusted patio furniture. He found a brick laying in the weeds and broke a window around back to gain entrance. He assumed the place was deserted because the front lawn was overgrown and there was a "For Sale" sign out front, but you never knew.

The gun felt unnaturally warm in his hand, but he was sure that was just his imagination, his guilty conscience.

It was clear others had been here before. There were a couple of mattresses in the otherwise bare living room and dozens of candles, most burned down to stumps, their wax dotting the wooden floor. The wax from various red candles looked like clotted blood, and that seemed like a bad omen, so he avoided looking at it.

There were remains of a fire in the fireplace, and, on the floor before it, a stack of pizza boxes, some empty beer bottles and a makeshift ashtray made out of a coffee can. On the bare mattress was a roach clip and a single sneaker.

These odds and ends comprised all the furnishings in the old place.

Not counting the drawings, of course. The walls were curiously free of spray paint and marker graffiti, but there were dozens of sketches in charcoal. They had a frenzied energy about them, and Johnny B thought they showed some sophistication.

He had thought of studying art history when he entered City College, but that was four years and several bad choices ago.

A quick check of the kitchen and downstairs bath confirmed that the place seemed vacant, but he knew Kix would be pissed if he didn't check the upstairs. Johnny B thought the guy might bleed out before he could check a place this big, but Kix had said he would kill Johnny B himself if there was anyone there.

It was a stupid plan, in Johnny B's opinion. Four of them had robbed a bank in nearby Lowell. Tucker had gotten away with most of the cash. Petrie had gotten shot by a security guard and Kix had gotten hit in the abdomen by the same guy. He would have bled out or ended up in prison if Johnny B hadn't put the guard down.

Which meant that all of them were now part of a murder as well as a robbery.

They had picked a couple of places to hole up and meet if things went sideways, and Kix had instructed Johnny B to text Tucker "PB," as in "Plan B", which was this dump. Johnny B thought it was very unlikely Tucker was going to meet them.

Johnny B wasn't not sure he would have, if he had the money. It's not like Kix had access to a vast intelligence network. Tucker could light out for Canada or Mexico and they'd never see him again.

Au revoir and *hasta la vista.*

If Johnny B had any guts (or sense, he thought miserably), he'd have dumped Kix in front of a hospital while he was passed out and then headed to the sticks... Maybe Iowa or something. Get a new identity and finish school, maybe teach or work on cars or something. After a couple of years he could probably stop looking over his shoulder, maybe even try living in France or the UK.

But that was a useless line of daydreaming, so he checked out the upstairs, which just featured another stained mattress and a room that smelled so foul he didn't go in. He was certain no human being could stay in such a room for long, unless they had a scuba suit or something.

There was no attic or basement that he could find, so Johnny B went out to collect the car and Kix. This reminded him that he hadn't checked the garage, but it was even emptier than the house. Seems like the local teens did not find it suitable for their illicit activities.

Johnny B left the garage door open and then went to fetch the car.

The entire street looked deserted. He could see Christmas lights a couple of blocks over, but all of the houses on this street were dark. It had been one of the finer neighborhoods in its day, but now the big homes were deserted and falling into disrepair. Some day the whole thing would probably be bulldozed for low cost housing or a shopping mall.

The car was a stolen Chevy Celebrity with switched plates and a hasty paint over with half a dozen cans of cobalt blue over the once-white vehicle. It looked like crap but wouldn't attract attention.

Kix was laying in the back. He looked pale and the towel he had pressed to his midsection was soaked through with blood. Johnny B was surprised he was alive, let alone conscious.

"Where the hell you been, kid?" Kix was actually a year younger than Johnny B, but always called him "kid." It firmly established their hierarchy, and Johnny B guessed it was better than having to call Kix "Boss," like some old Cagney movie.

"Had to check out the house, like you asked." Johnny B put the slightest edge on the second part of that sentence, and slid behind the wheel.

"Bet you were hopin' to find me dead, huh?"

Johnny B could tell Kix was watching him intently, he could see the glint of the other man's weasel eyes in the rearview. "That's not true and you know it, Kix. We've been friends a long time."

"Forget it, kid, I'm just busting your chops. Tucker isn't there yet, is he?"

Tucker's half way to Puerto Vallarta or Quebec, Johnny B thought, but said nothing.

Johnny B parked the car in the garage and closed it, and then helped Kix through the adjoining door into the kitchen. From there it was just a short walk to the mattress in the living room. Johnny B spotted a balled up sweater on the far side of the mattress and gave this to Kix as a makeshift bandage.

As far as he could tell, Kix had no exit wound, which meant the slug was still inside him. If he didn't bleed to death or develop sepsis from the filthy bandages, the bullet would probably do him in.

Kix moaned as Johnny B removed the blood-soaked towel and replaced it with the sweater, a pink thing with a little butterfly clip over the left breast.

"We gotta get you to a doctor, man."

Kix shook his head. "Gotta be here when Tucker gets here."

Johnny B had a momentary image of Tucker drinking Mexican beer in a beach chair, then pushed the traitorous thought from his mind.

While Johnny B made Kix as comfortable as possible, he could see the big man struggling to stay awake. If Kix fell asleep, he could just leave. He could even make a call to 911 from a payphone and tell them a man with a gunshot wound was clinging to life in this godforsaken dump. Kix would go to jail, but he would be alive.

Alive on death row, anyway.

There was a thump from the garage and he could see that Kix was awake and alert. He gestured with his head that Johnny B should check it out.

Johnny B was wondering what his chances might be to slip out the back and go over the fence, when the door to the kitchen opened slowly.

Feeling slightly nauseous, Johnny B drew his gun and

pointed it at the doorway. If he killed a cop, then it would be a lethal injection for sure, but what choice did he have?

"That you, John-Boy?" a voice asked from the darkness of the garage.

Tucker looked in, and Johnny B's entire body shook with relief and unused adrenaline.

Tucker had not only brought the money, but had grabbed some supplies from a bodega several blocks away. Coverage of the robbery had been on the television, and it was clear that all of them were masked and that the police, despite making comments to the contrary, had no leads.

Tucker made them baloney sandwiches with mustard and lettuce on white bread, but Kix could only nibble a bit of the crust. He was pale and sweating, and Johnny B knew he wouldn't last more than a day or two at this rate. Part of him was glad, because he blamed Kix for the life he was leading. Another part was worried, because he was sure the police would tie Kix to the robbery, and him to Kix.

Kix drank some of the Jack Daniels that Tucker had brought, then slipped into an uneasy sleep.

In the kitchen, Tucker and Johnny B talked in low tones.

"He looks bad, John-Boy."

Johnny B hated being called John-Boy. He liked Johnny B, with its reference to "Johnny B. Goode" by Chuck Barry. He knew Tucker said it just to needle him, and if he didn't react Tucker might stop, but Johnny B could never keep a slight look of annoyance from crossing his features, and that was all Tucker needed. Now, in spite of their situation, in spite of everything,

Johnny B saw that same self-satisfied smile cross Tucker's face and he hated him for it.

But they had Kix to worry about, so he let it slide.

"I think the bullet's still in his abdomen. We need to get someone here who can get it out."

"Doctors have to report gunshot wounds, you know that. Besides, do you know any doctors who would be willing to do it?"

Johnny B shook his head.

"Nurse? Intern?"

Again, Johnny B shook his head.

"Hell," said Tucker, "I don't even know a veterinarian."

"Well, we can't do it," Johnny B said, "we'd kill him for sure."

Tucker motioned behind him toward the living room. "We got close to half a million in cash," he said. "Split two ways that's two-fifty each."

Johnny B gaped, even though similar thoughts had been running through his head earlier, and without the extra-added attraction of cash.

"You want to... you want to just leave him here?"

"Not the way he is," Tucker whispered.

And Johnny B understood that Tucker meant that they needed to make sure the one witness who could identify them positively was not found alive.

"No," Johnny B said, backing up a step. He had only killed one person in his life and wanted never to do it again, not even by his inaction.

Now a new look came into Tucker's head, some new calculation about one extra bullet buying him another $250K.

Johnny B was just thinking about trying the back door when the kitchen door swung in and then Kix was firing and Tucker shrieked and went down, his blood spreading quickly on the dirty gray linoleum.

Kix looked at Johnny B, seeming to, in that moment, read his thoughts. Johnny B was sure he was going to die, and a thought came to him unbidden of a girl he sat behind in History of Modern Art. He had never learned her name, but she had smelled like soap and flowers and Roma Plastilina clay.

Kix lowered the gun. "I know you won't cross me, kid. "

Johnny B, realizing he was going to live, nodded rapidly.

"Help me back to the mattress, kid... Killing that bastard used up any reserves I had left."

Johnny B got him back, and Kix winced as he laid down.

"Kix, do you know anyone who can patch you up?"

"No. Guess getting shot was never part of my plan." Kix laughed, but it sounded forced and ended in a wheezing cough.

"There's no way you can travel any more, Kix. And I think that bullet is still inside you."

"When did you start attending medical school, kid? If I had known, I would've gotten you a stethoscope for Christmas."

"I didn't see an exit wound, is all."

"Ah, so you're CSI, now. I'll get ya a microscope."

Johnny B shook his head, the gravity of their situation becoming greater with every minute.

"Plus we've got a dead body in the kitchen."

"I know that!" Kix snapped, then quieted. "We're not going to solve any of these problems right now. Let's get some sleep and figure it out in a couple of hours or so. I'm done in, kid."

Johnny B wanted to protest that they didn't have a couple of hours, that darkness was their ally, right now. But it was only going on 6 pm and he was weary; the adrenaline surges of the last few hours had left him almost shaking with fatigue.

Johnny B used the money bag as a pillow, and kept his gun ready in his jacket pocket. He heard Kix's breathing slow, and knew that the big man was asleep.

Johnny B thought he heard Christmas music off in the distance. One of the hymns, maybe "O Come, All Ye Faithful." He had liked that one as a kid. He knew it was probably his imagination, but maybe there was a church nearby.

It was Christmas Eve, and the thought brought him no joy. Right now his sister and her family would be preparing for the big day, maybe watching those holiday specials they had seen a hundred times. Their Mom might be visiting from Arizona. He wasn't sure, but it seemed like more than two years since he had actually talked to them.

How had it gotten so far out of control? So far from what he thought his life would be?

He had hoped to transfer to UCLA in his junior year, get a scholarship and become an art or art history teacher until his own career paid the bills.

But a professor had trashed his portfolio early in his sophomore year, calling it "amateurish and trite."

He should have gotten angry and tried harder, or at the very least, realized that one person's opinion does not make a career. But he had always been told he was a natural, that his self-taught abilities were going to take him to giddying heights in galleries and museums.

He started skipping classes, and met Kix and Tucker at a chili dog stand. The two were arguing over the merits of an action film and Johnny B couldn't help chiming in.

If only I had kept my mouth shut, or gone to class that day...

But he hadn't, and he had been led on by the promise of adventure and easy money, and the notion that he could pick up a brush any time, and it would be all the easier because he would have money, money to do whatever he had wanted.

And so they began robbing small businesses, and then houses. Banks had always been on the horizon of Kix's master plan, and soon they grew cocky and to think they were invincible.

And now, here they were, three men dead counting the guard and another dying, with barely enough food and water for a week, if that.

Leave, he thought, *just ease into the garage and take the car and go.*

He could do it. He could turn it all around, given time. Maybe the guard hadn't died, he wasn't a hundred percent positive he had killed him. And the guard, unlike Kix, had likely had proper medical attention.

But if he left Kix here, wouldn't that be tantamount to

murder? The man had lost a lot of blood. But what could he do about it? If he called 911 on his way out of town, they would get to Kix and maybe he would live.

Finally, Johnny B fell asleep, his problems unresolved.

He slept fitfully, waking several times thinking he had heard an odd, scratching sound from somewhere in the house.

Maybe it was a cat trying to get in, he thought, and went back to sleep.

He had a terrible nightmare. In it, he had heard the scratching again, only this time it was definitely coming from the kitchen. Drawing his gun, he had gone slowly to the door, the living room bathed in the silver light of a full moon.

The scratching continued, and he eased open the door.

Tucker was scratching to get in, like a dog. But he was dead, and his eyes were solid white that glowed with a faint, flickering luminosity.

As Tucker reached out for him, Johnny B had awakened with a start. He was sweating and breathing hard, but he hadn't wakened Kix.

Johnny B shook his head and shifted the money bag, which was only slightly better than the wooden floor as a pillow.

Tucker was looking at him

Ha, he used to feel like that as a kid. That if he turned around, the figure of his nightmare would be waiting for him, to grab him and take him far from his home and snug little bed.

Tucker is watching you - he's right behind you

This was stupid. What was he, twelve? There weren't any

boogeymen, just idiots who dropped out of school and used a gun instead of their brains.

Tucker wants you to join him

And then there came the scratching sound, and it was right behind him.

Johnny B never thought of himself as particularly brave, but he did turn around that night.

And Tucker was looking at him.

Johnny B almost screamed, because Tucker's eyes were wide and clearly dead, and he seemed to be hanging upside-down in the fireplace, like a bat or a vampire from some old drive-in movie.

The scratching came again, and then Tucker disappeared up the chimney.

…like Santa Claus

That was a creepy thought, and Johnny B put it right out of his mind.

He was delirious. Hell, maybe he was still dreaming. Maybe there was some kind of mold in the house that was hallucinogenic. Didn't he see that on the History Channel one time?

But this was real. Which was crazy, because living men couldn't go up chimneys like some dime store vampire, let alone dead ones.

You know Tucker is still lying in the kitchen, right?

He decided he wasn't going to give into his childish fears and made himself sleep.

Johnny B woke in the gray light of Christmas morning, needing to relieve himself. He looked over and saw that Kix was still out, his breathing loud and ragged.

Johnny B wanted to hate the big man, but that was dodging responsibility, wasn't it? It was too early to get into this now; his eyes felt like they were filled with coarse sand and his mouth tasted like he had been chewing on old socks.

There was a bathroom, but no water. He used the toilet, trying not to breathe. He tried the tap, just to be sure, but nothing came out.

Johnny B came back into the living room, and stopped.

The light in the living room was pearlescent, and strong enough for him to see that someone had worked on the charcoal sketches over Kix's head.

Someone had added bright splashes and spots of red.

A red that was turning brown.

Then, without really wanting to, Johnny looked at the kitchen. There was a bright crimson swath, like someone had dragged a bloody mop across the floor. It continued past where he had been sleeping and into the fireplace.

He could see his footprints where he had stepped in the blood and tracked it.

"What are you lookin' at, kid?"

Johnny B was about to point at the blood when a bristling black horror scuttled out of the chimney, across the wall and latched onto Kix.

Kix screamed as the thing grabbed him, and it scuttled up

the wall as if he weighed nothing, leaving frenetic marks of charcoal and ash, and small droplets of blood.

Johnny B pulled his gun, then looked into the things eyes, eyes like beads of oil, that registered a queer and alien intelligence.

Go

The voice sounded in his head, and he realized he was being given a second chance.

Johnny B grabbed the money, and the last thing he heard was Kix cursing him as he was dragged up into the chimney to join Tucker.

Johnny B kept just enough money to get out of town and scrounge some meals. He bought a bus ticket for Kansas City, Missouri, then dropped off the rest of the money at a local church. It seemed like the right thing to do.

As the bus pulled out of the Greyhound station, he placed a call to his sister, wondering just what he would say once he got past "Merry Christmas."

SANTA VS. DRACULA

Dracula had had it.

He prided himself on being the Prince of Darkness, The Scourge of Transylvania, the bloodthirsty count who terrorized mortals the world over.

To know his name was to know fear: Vlad Dracul... Dracula!

And yet, every Christmas people refused to lock their doors at sunset and cower inside. They waited for the coming of his mortal enemy.

Santa Claus.

Oh, how he hated that name!

Well, no more, he decided. Tonight he would pass his curse on to the most beloved figure in childhood, and his reign of terror would reach epic proportions.

The Count had been watching a particular neighborhood in Muskool, Ohio, looking for the best boy or girl.

He knew people would expect him to be in some major metropolitan area wreaking havoc, but a town of less than five-thousand?

Not bloody likely.

He finally chose Megan Collier, who was five and an insufferable goody-goody.

At just before midnight, he turned into a fog and drifted under the front door, then reassumed his dread shape. He noted with disgust the Christmas tree, the stockings over the fireplace, the glass of milk and plate of cookies with M&M's baked into them. Dracula thought of spitting into the milk, but didn't want to alert The Kringle to his presence.

He crept quietly as a cat into the room of Megan Collier. He tripped over the child's backpack, but swiftly changed into a bat and didn't crash into any furniture.

Regaining human form, he listened for any sounds of alarm.

There were none.

Then, as silently and deadly as marsh gas, he slipped into Megan's closet and waited.

Inside the Count's supernatural eyesight adjusted instantly to the dark and he saw that the closet was filled with princess outfits and stuffed toy unicorns with big, trusting eyes.

The Count sighed unhappily, but stayed hidden.

He could hear the child just outside the door sleeping

peacefully. Oh, how he wanted to creep out of the closet and scare her! Then feed on her, biting and...

"Come out of there, Count."

It was a deep voice, stern and commanding. Certainly no little girl.

Dracula prepared himself to do battle and exited the closet. Instantly, he was seized by several of Santa's elves. They were small but surprisingly strong, and held him fast.

Santa approached him, and wagged a pudgy finger. "Vlad Dracul! I used to bring you sugar cookies, turta dulce and wooden swords... Now look at you, on the Permanent Naughty List!"

"Then go ahead and kill me, Kringle!" Dracula snarled. "Your reputation will be ruined and I shall triumph!"

Santa laughed. "I am not going to kill you, you bad boy - I am going to rehabilitate you, acclimate you to a diet of gingerbread and cocoa... By the time we are finished, every child will love you and call you Uncle Drac or Cousin Batty."

"Never!" the vampire spat. "With my fangs I will lay waste to your workshop and all your -- "

"Yes, yes," said Santa, clearly unimpressed. He gestured to a tiny woman only two feet high. She had iridescent wings and carried a giant pair of pliers.

"Have you met my friend, The Tooth Fairy?"

THE TINKER'S TALE

By now you have heard of the Red Lion tavern and inn, a place unparalleled for its fare, its comfortable beds, and the hospitality of its hosts, Helmut and Gerta Zauberwald and their beautiful daughter Dorothea.

Of all that patronized that fine establishment, none was seen as often as Anders Bergin, a tinker who had wandered into the region and decided to stay. It wasn't just because Anders had a prodigious thirst for ale, and the uncanny ability to get others to pay for his drinks. He was an excellent listener, and the Red Lion was the best place in the whole of the Black Forest to learn things – important things.

Things like, what fine family might be leaving their house unattended to attend a royal wedding.

Or, what route a shipment of gold might be taking.

Or where a widow might hide her jewels.

Truth be told, Anders Bergin was a terrible tinker but an excellent thief. If he could not steal something himself, he sold the information to other thieves.

In this way, he did very well and only mended the occasional pot or pan to keep his real occupation secret. The repair job was usually so poor and slipshod that he was rarely rehired. That was all right, for what could be more natural than a talentless tinker whiling away his hours in a tavern?

Of course, much of what he heard was drivel. Pure superstition that often passed for fact among the peasantry, especially in remote locations like this.

Werewolves.

Witches.

Trolls.

Vampires.

It was all tripe and Anders was far too smart to be taken in by stories of houses of gingerbread and maidens in glass coffins.

However, he did know that some old tales contained a kernel of truth. He too had heard tales of the *Lutzelfrau*, the Yule Witch, who demanded small gifts in winter and would sometimes grant a boon. Anders reasoned that some woman posing as such a creature might collect a tidy sum from foolish peasants and superstitious country folk.

While Anders enjoyed a hearty Christmas Eve dinner with Helmut and his family, as well as Gustav the woodcutter and Jürgen the Huntsman, he casually mentioned the *Lutzelfrau*. He was surprised to see a guilty look pass between Helmut and his wife Gerta.

So they had fallen for the old wives' tales, and now were embarrassed about their naiveté. Anders asked if anyone knew where such a woman lived, and all Helmut would say was that he had "heard" she lived somewhere in the middle of the forest.

After dinner, Anders begged off spending the night, and noticed with some amusement Gerta trying to disguise her relief. He was surprised to see he would have company on the road for a ways, as the young man Peter who had been en route to Munich was also leaving. Anders was sure that the young man was sweet on Helmut's daughter, but perhaps the host of the Red Lion was not so welcoming or cordial when it came to matters concerning his only child.

The two rode in silence and he could see the young man was nervous. It occurred to Anders that the young man was probably planning on eloping with young Dorothea, and that perhaps he should stop this. Such interference would probably earn him a lifetime of gratitude from the innkeeper and his wife. But Anders already got most of his drinks (and quite a few of his meals) for free. The only thing he might fancy was the girl herself, and she had already made it clear that she found him repugnant. Oh, it was something she tried to disguise behind smiles and stray bits of song, but Anders knew the signs. So let her try and make her way with this young oaf. If they were robbed by highwaymen or ended up out on the streets and penniless, neither was his affair.

At the fork they parted company, Peter continuing on the main road out of the forest. Anders rode on, but dismounted just beyond a bend and then skulked back and watched the road from the cover of darkness. Sure enough, fifteen minutes later the boy rode slowly back, looked about for Anders, then rode back toward the Red Lion.

People were so predictable.

Anders stopped an hour later to rest his horse and eat a bit of late supper. He was carving some meat from a ham shank when a gnarled old woman emerged from the wood. She was dressed in rough homespun and smelled of mildew and age.

"Happy Christmas to you, sir," she said, managing a clumsy curtsy.

Anders merely nodded at her, and took a drink of ale.

The old woman licked her lips. She was nearly toothless and her chin had several coarse hairs sticking out of it. She was the ugliest creature Anders had ever seen.

"Sir, might I impose on you for a slice of meat, a crust of bread?"

Anders chewed and thought, then motioned with his knife, his mouth still full of food. "I'll do you one better, grandmother, tell me where I can find the *Lutzelfrau* and I will throw in some ale, as well."

The old woman gazed longingly at the food, like a dog at a butcher shop's back door. She wrung her hands, clearly in distress, then said, "I know of no such person, good sir."

Anders shrugged, then threw a bit of fat and gristle into the fire. She scrambled for it and burned herself as she snatched it from the flames and threw it onto the snow bank. She ate it greedily and with a great amount of noise. Anders looked away, disgusted by her display. When he turned back, she peered at him, hopeful.

"A small sip of your ale, good sir, or perhaps a coin on this Christmas Eve?"

"Be gone, old woman, you've gotten all the supper you'll receive from me this night. Tarry longer and I'll make a present of my boot to your backside."

The old woman scuttled off into the forest and was gone.

It occurred to him that such a woman might be working with robbers in the area. That was no matter; Anders had a good knife and short sword, and he was proficient in the use of both. He had traveled through cities like Munich at night alone, certainly he was not afraid of this overgrown garden called the Black Forest.

He moved on, deeper into the woods. He heard odd movements in the underbrush. Once or twice he even thought he heard whispering, loud enough to make out words, but they were in some language he had never heard before.

Just before midnight he heard a branch split, and then a crash followed by a scream. Anders would never admit it to any living soul, but by now he was terrified. He dismounted quickly and tethered his horse behind a large deadfall and waited.

Then came a sound like the crunching of bone and Anders believed he could smell blood in the air, a great deal of it, and the odor made him sick. He fought his rising gorge, lest he give away his hiding place.

Something strode through the clearing, something easily twenty feet tall. It was gripping something bleeding and broken in its great hands, and Anders could not tell if the dead thing it carried was a cow or a man or something altogether different.

His horse snorted in fear and he held his breath as he tried to quiet the animal. The giant creature turned toward him, and he saw two large eyes glowing with witch lights, and a suggestion of great, sharp tusks. It sniffed the air once, then went on its way, making little noise for something so huge, and that was also disturbing.

Anders waited another ten minutes, almost certain that something worse would be following the thing – was it a giant? a troll? - but the forest was eerily silent.

He rode for another hour and came at last upon a small cottage, and knew intuitively that he had reached his destination. The place was dark, save for a golden glow coming from the barn.

As he was heading toward the barn, an old woman called to him from the door of the hut.

"Happy Christmas to you, traveler. Do you seek lodging for your horse?"

He turned, affecting his most ingratiating smile. "Happy Christmas to you, dear lady. I am looking for the *Lutzelfrau*."

"Then I would say your quest is at an end. Would you enter and share a cup of tea with me? Perhaps a slice of bread?"

"Yes, and I would thank you." Anders removed a saddle bag and brought it in with him.

Where the hut seemed dark before, it was now ablaze with light, a cheery fire in the fireplace and candles in every corner. Though he saw some dried herbs and old books, there was nothing of the usual props and geegaws one associated with witches.

The old woman poured them each a steaming cup, and he saw that she was the oldest woman he had ever seen. Her hair was white and thin, her face and hands wrinkled and gnarled like ancient tree bark. She was stooped but moved easily enough, seemingly free of the afflictions which old age usually brings with it like a suitor with gifts for a beloved.

She retrieved a half loaf of bread from the pantry, and it looked much like the bread served by Helmut in the Red Lion.

"Not much of a Christmas dinner, I fear," she said regretfully, yet he thought he traced some hint of merriment in her eyes.

"If you would share with me, good mother, I have some ham from an inn I frequent."

"How kind of you to share with an old woman, a stranger," she said, and again he thought he detected a twinkle in her gaze, a sense that she was mocking him.

He thought of the old peasant woman on the road, but dismissed this. That woman had been coarse and rude. This woman might be old but still had a bearing of nobility, of breeding.

They ate, and the old woman proved to have a tremendous appetite. She ate most of the ham and the bread. Anders was happy he had eaten earlier.

At last there was nothing left but bone and crumbs, and she wiped her face daintily with a bit of old linen.

"Now then, traveler, what would you ask of me?"

He remembered from his boyhood that no sorcerer had power over you as long as you didn't give your true name. He had been ready to give a false name if necessary, and chided himself for his foolishness. She hadn't even asked him who he was. As he had suspected, she was no witch, but a huckster, much like himself.

But he was stronger, quicker, and good with a blade. Confident, his prize nearly won, he grinned at her. On some men a smile brings a pleasant aspect, but Anders Bergin was not such a man.

"I'd like all the gold you have collected playing at being the Yule Witch."

She laughed, and it sounded genuine. Anders continued to smile as she quieted.

"Ah, traveler, I'll warrant that is the first honest thing you have said in many a day. And, if I refuse, will you use your knife on me, or perhaps your sword?"

He felt a moment's hesitation, and then realized that she may have seen into his bag when he retrieved the ham shank, or she might even be bluffing.

"Yes."

She considered him, and now her cold regard did make him anxious.

"I will do you one better, Anders Bergin," she said.

She knows my name! Good Lord, she is a witch! Get out, get out! He fought to calm his mind and rebuked himself for falling prey to superstition.

"I will give you a gift," she said. "One worth many pounds of gold."

"Do not trifle with me, old woman; I will not leave here with some worthless talisman or supposedly enchanted beans."

She laughed. "I suppose you would not, though such things have their worth." She got up and went to a cupboard.

Anders watched her closely, lest she retrieve a weapon.

She brought out a small chest, and set it on the table. He watched it warily, sure that there might be a poisonous creature within.

She chuckled as if reading his thoughts and opened the box. Anders drew back involuntarily, thinking of snakes and loathsome creatures like venomous toads.

Something glowed brightly within the box, and now he thought it might be gold or gems catching the candlelight.

She reached into the chest and brought forth a small lantern, such as a child might carry, and set it on the table.

Anders stared.

There, within, was a tiny woman, dressed in flower petals and with iridescent wings like a dragonfly. She glowed, flickering like a candle flame as she flitted within the confines of her glass prison.

"What is it?" he whispered.

"Why, it's the Sugar Plum Fairy," the *Lutzelfrau* answered.

Anders looked up at her, trying to find that glint of amusement in her eyes, but the old hag seemed to be speaking the truth.

He looked down, trying to deny the truth he was seeing with his own eyes. True, he might be dreaming, but his dreams had never been this remarkable.

"She would fetch a fortune in Munich," he exclaimed.

"True, but…"

Now he glared at the old woman. "Don't try and withhold this from me, old woman, or it will go badly for you."

She raised a hand.

"I merely want to suggest that her people are looking for her, and will reward anyone who returns her."

"With gold? I have no use for a fairy treasure that will disappear when I am clear of these benighted woods."

"I give you my word that their gold is real."

"It had better be, old mother, or I will come back and take anything of value and leave you to whatever predators call this land home."

The old woman nodded, and told him to head two leagues due east.

Anders took the lantern and went to his horse. The old woman followed him. "Mind you, get her back before the dawn. Sunlight can kill fairies."

Anders saw the glow again from the barn, and thought to himself that two fortunes were certainly worth more than one.

Quick as a snake, he withdrew the knife from his belt and stabbed the old woman in the ribs. She gasped and went down, and he wiped the blade on her skirts.

Anders went into the barn and found several bags of gold and jewels. There were more than he could carry on his horse, and so he resolved to bury them and retrieve them later. First, he would deliver the fairy to her people and collect his reward.

He rode east as instructed, and the trees began to take on strange and twisted shapes, as if they had been poisoned as saplings. He saw several night birds, but they seemed to have too many wings and their cries were too close to human speech, seeming to cry "Murderer" and "Thief." Anders put this down to his guilty conscience and superstitious childhood and rode on.

At last, through the trees, he saw small lights moving to and fro, and the fairy within his lantern beat against the glass with her wings and tiny fists.

"Welcome home, Princess," he whispered.

He rode into the clearing and found it dark, lit only by starlight. Anders held up the lantern.

"I have brought you a gift, little people, come and wish me 'Happy Christmas'!"

Slowly little lights appeared, like fireflies alight on every branch, root and stone.

Tiny men and women, winged and glowing, gathered around him until it was as bright as day within the glade.

Several feinted at the lantern and he waved them back with his knife.

"I do not know your kind, but I am fairly certain a silvered blade would kill or maim your princess."

He saw their pretty faces turn angry, and mustered his courage. He was so close.

"I would take whatever gold and riches you have," he said. Then, inspiration hit him. "You will carry all that gold and the gold in the barn of the *Lutzelfrau* to my home. Only then will I release you."

Anders Bergin.

The voice came from inside his head and some intuition caused him to look into the eyes of the Sugar Plum Fairy.

Two gifts I give you for my return – the first was to see us, as children dream of us... This you have done...

Anders realized something was terribly wrong and wanted to run, but his legs seemed fixed and immobile.

The other, to see us as cruel and wicked men do... This I give you now.

There was a shift in the air, a ripple through the glade, and the fairy folk changed.

Some tales will tell you that to see the fairy folk in this aspect is to invite madness, but that is not entirely true. Madness can bring relief, and there was none for Ander Bergin that night.

The scaled and spiny creatures that assailed him, all spider's eyes and wasp stingers, have been hinted at in paintings of demons and imps from the infernal regions. Yet I must tell you such imagined creatures pale in comparison to the leprous and fanged monstrosities that attacked the Tinker that Christmas night.

Be thankful knowing that, whatever you have imagined, it cannot compare with the horrors of the Black Forest.

After several days, the *Lutzelfrau* found fresh bits of bone on her path to the barn, and the Tinker's horse inside, both gifts from the fairy folk. She sent the horse on his way, knowing he would find his way to the Red Lion and be well cared for there.

Later, she would travel to the Lake of the Restless Dead, where many ghosts howl and wail in chorus with the winter wind. She would go to visit with the Sugar Plum Fairy, and tell her what transpired after the Tinker left her bleeding in the dooryard of her home.

But that is a tale for another day.

CHRISTMAS, THE OLD WAY

Every Christmas we come down from the crumbling and mold-ridden shops and homes of our town to the black and heaving sea, where our relatives emerge from the waves with presents, special delicacies, and toys fashioned for the young ones of bone and coral, shell and gem.

For our part, we bring nameless things from the forests and mountains, and toys for the young ones of bone and stone, wood and web.

Then we feast for an entire week on black widow egg wine and squid ink lager, heaping trays of venomous vermin and poisonous rockfish. We stuff ourselves on raw eels and frisky beetles, and eat shark-eye pie and hornet sting cakes.

Finally, the big day comes, and the youngest are tricked out in all the finery we have brought in large trunks from the caves and foot lockers from the sea. They dance and flap and caper about, their clothes the only human thing about them, and our aunts and uncles play eerie music on bone flutes and bladder drums and we all laugh and sing the old songs.

And, come midnight on Christmas Eve, we all look to the skies, waiting for the first jingling of bells.

And at last, we hear them!

My sister starts to cry and I sweep her up in my clumsy arms, my fused fingers making it difficult, but I hold her up and kiss her, and comfort her in the guttural tongue of joy.

And then, enormous tentacles covered in bells descend from the roiling clouds above, and seize, one, two, three... Four, five, six, my sister among them!

They are hoisted into the clouds and we dance until dawn, then fall into exhausted sleep under slick oilcloth tarps and overturned skiffs, safe from the punishing sun.

Later, as we dine on the traditional breakfast of jellyfish puddings and bear lung pasties, their pulverized bones rain down from high above, and it is... just... like... snow.

THE HUNTSMAN'S TALE

All who patronized the Red Lion Tavern and Inn came to know the Huntsman by sight, but few actually knew anything about him.

Even those who shared an ale with him could only tell you that his first name was Jürgen and that he lived somewhere in the Black Forest. Others might add that the severe scar that ran from his forehead, over the bridge of his nose and creating a divide in one cheek was not from an animal but from a man. Some said this occurred in war, when Jürgen protected the virtue of a young maid from his own fellows. But just where the war had taken place (and when) were details no one seemed privy to.

Truth be told, the Huntsman was a man of few words and chose not to spend that meager output on himself. Unlike Anders the Tinker, the Huntsman was loathe to share any tales about himself, even those that might earn him a stein of drink or a meal from his rapt listeners.

Of friends he only had two, Helmut the Innkeeper and Gustav the Woodcutter. And although he would not be so presumptuous as to call them friends, he also held Helmut's wife and daughter in high esteem.

He had heard from Gustav that there was a poacher in the Black Forest, a man who used cruel traps rather than the more honorable weapons of knife and bow.

Jürgen set out to find the man (or men) and confront them. He considered the Black Forest his home and could not abide poachers, whom he considered no better than thieves.

He knew such men would probably lay their traps at night, under the cover of darkness. After dining at the Red Lion with his friends – well, except for Anders the Tinker, whom he had never quite trusted – Jürgen set out to trap cunning game of his own.

In a clearing not far from the home of Gustav the Woodcutter, he found blood in the snow and evidence that a trap had been pulled up. Tracks that were almost certainly Gustav's led back toward his cottage, while wolf tracks went off into the forest, the bleeding animal favoring one front leg.

It was not an easy thing to free a wolf. He must remind himself to buy Gustav a drink the next time they were in the Red Lion.

Though the scene had been disturbed greatly, Jürgen was able to discern tracks of a different individual; tracks he suspected belonged to the poacher. He followed these for several miles, nearly losing the trail a number of times. It was clear his quarry was also an expert and good at hiding his tracks.

After three hours, Jürgen could smell the aroma of rabbit

being cooked on an open fire. He came to a copse of old growth pine, deep within the darkest heart of the forest. There he spied a caravan wagon and two horses. Sitting before a small, smokeless fire was a large and bald man with a patch over one eye.

Jürgen noted the man had a loaded crossbow within easy reach, and called out before entering the stranger's campsite.

"Heil, stranger," he called.

The man had obviously heard him coming, for he did not seem surprised at Jürgen's greeting.

"Heil," he answered. "If you have come looking for a meal I am afraid I've but one small rabbit, and he is mostly bones, now."

Jürgen stepped into the clearing. "No matter and I thank you just the same. I ate earlier at the Red Lion."

The stranger nodded and chewed a last bit of meat from a bone.

"I am called Jürgen van Vogt," he offered.

The stranger nodded but did not give his name, nor did he seem inclined to pass the time in conversation.

"I've come about the traps," said Jürgen, and now the man did look up.

"This forest is under my protection and others like me," said Jürgen, realizing he might have to dodge a crossbow bolt any second, now.

"And the hellspawn that infest this forest?" asked the one-eyed man. "Are they under your protection, as well?"

"This is an ancient realm," said Jürgen, "It was old before

Men arrived. We have our peace with the night creatures. They leave us alone. In exchange, anyone stupid enough to blunder into their lands is fair game."

The stranger laughed. "Really, and you expect them to hold to such a contract?"

"Aye, and hold it they have. If you are meaning to trap something other than game I will take issue with that, as well. It's a delicate balance here, and someone like you may upset our peaceful coexistence."

The stranger gestured at his eyepatch. "Shifter, in Britain. I'll have no truck with those bastards, despite what you say, Herr Jürgen van Vogt, guardian of the Black Forest."

"And I say you have obviously had your vengeance, if the pelt affixed to your wagon is any indication."

At this the man grinned and threw a bone into the fire.

"I will give you a day to move on," Jürgen continued. "If you care to come to the Red Lion, I will even buy you a drink, one Huntsman to another. But your poaching in my forest is done."

The stranger merely nodded, but that in itself was not an agreement.

Jürgen backed out of the clearing, his hand never far from one of his knives, but the stranger made no provocative moves.

# #

Jürgen noticed that both his friend Helmut and Gustav seemed troubled in those days after Christmas, but his offers to help or lend any kind of aid were politely refused. Being a man who prided himself on reading the smallest signs in the wild, he knew there were secrets being kept, and knew that they were not his business. Soon both men regained their cheerful demeanor, and the Red Lion became even livelier with the addition of young Peter to the staff. Jürgen imagined there would be a wedding soon, and silently wished Dorothea and her young man well.

Anders the Tinker stopped coming in, and no one at the Red Lion was sorry at his absence. Those acquainted with him knew him as a braggart and a liar and very probably a thief. But then a representative of the Prince came to the inn, claiming Anders had shamed a royal cousin, and was to appear before his majesty in order to answer to such an affront.

Jürgen had no wish for the Prince and his men to tromp through the forest, scaring away game and perhaps exciting the Black Forest's "other" population. He offered to track Anders and bring him in personally. The tracking skills of Jürgen van Vogt were legendary and the Prince's representative promised him a fine reward upon delivery of the Tinker.

It did not take Jürgen long to find the trail of Anders, and his route was going to take him not far from the encampment of the one-eyed stranger. Jürgen decided to stop there and see if his warning had been heeded.

He approached the campsite and could see the wagon through the trees. Although there was no meal cooking, he could smell something.

Blood. A great deal of it.

Jürgen approached slowly. The horses were gone, and he could see they had been untied and presumably let loose. The campfire circle was filled with snow – indeed, the entire area was virgin snow without a single track or boot print.

And still that odor of blood…

Jürgen tethered his horse and went cautiously to the caravan's entrance at the back. He noted that the pelt that had been there before was gone. His knife at the ready, he entered.

Inside, it was a charnel house, with every surface painted in blood. Jürgen almost wondered if there might be more than one victim, because the walls ran thick with it. The smell was nauseating and he had to make himself step in just far enough to deduce there was no body.

On the far side of the caravan, there was a pelt of an altogether different sort, and a single word in blood:

MURDERER.

Jürgen decided to leave the wagon as a warning to others who might want to follow in the one-eyed man's footsteps. That one word, painted in the poacher's blood, was a far more eloquent warning than any Jürgen might issue.

He returned to his horse and again followed the trail of Anders the Tinker, wondering if he had had any dealings with the one-eyed man. It seemed likely, and he also wondered if Anders might have had a hand in the death of the stranger, although Anders had never struck him as someone who gave a damn about the forest or its people.

He traveled deeper into the forest, a place most men did not dare go, but Jürgen did not hesitate. He had forged alliances with some of the *Nachtsleute* and knew which others he should steer clear of.

He reached a cottage, one he had never seen, and spied an old woman unconscious at the threshold. Jürgen rushed to her, unmindful of traps or ambush.

She was the oldest woman he had ever seen, and some blackguard had stabbed her in the ribs. Luckily, the blade had not pierced any organs or major blood vessels, but she had lost a lot of blood. And deep in the forest there was also the danger of sepsis, which could kill as surely as a crossbow bolt or hand axe.

He got her inside and onto a small bed in the rear of the small cottage. She muttered something he did not understand.

"Quiet, old mother, let me see to your wound."

He had packed a small cask of wine and a bottle of whiskey, both of which could be effective bargaining tools with giants and some of the Cyclops. He soaked a rag in the whiskey and cleansed her wound with it, and the old woman hissed and cursed like a whoremaster.

Jürgen laughed. "I was worried about whether you had the strength to live – now I think you may outlive me."

He went out and fetched some moss from a nearby tree to make a poultice, but she waved it away when he tried to apply it.

"It's medicine, old woman, let me dress your wound!"

She pointed to a leather bag hanging near a shelf of ancient books and he brought it to her. Inside was a muslin bag that was terribly foul smelling, so much so that Jürgen nearly gagged.

"Surely this is poison," he remarked.

"Place it on my wound, you impertinent pup, and bind it tightly."

Jürgen did as she asked and only hesitated when the small bundle tried to wiggle away from her wound. But he was a brave man and had seen many strange things, and so he bound it tightly where it squirmed against the woman's skin like a trapped animal.

Then he made her a cup of weak broth, and this she drank without argument.

By midnight she was asleep, and Jürgen welcomed in Silvester, or the New Year, in the tiny cottage deep in the forest.

The old woman was stronger the next day and asked him his name.

"I am Jürgen von Vogt, old mother."

"I am in your debt, Jürgen von Vogt. I am the one they call the *Lutzelfrau*."

"The Yule Witch? I wasn't sure you actually existed."

"And yet, here I am," she said.

"I have seen and heard much in this forest," Jürgen continued, "but I have not seen you until now."

"I try to avoid people when I can," she said. "Those determined to find me will do so… Sometimes at their peril."

"And the one who did this?"

"I can take you to him, if you like."

"Is he still alive?"

She smiled in a way that let him know he wasn't.

"Then I am in no hurry," he said, "and you must rest."

"Again I thank you. May I ask what brings you to my home, Jürgen von Vogt?"

"I was tracking a miscreant who has wronged the Prince."

"Ah, so you are loyal to the Prince."

"I would say, rather, that I will do what I can to have this forest free of the tromping oafs under his majesty's command."

She smiled, then yawned and winced.

"Sleep now," he urged. "We can talk more when you are rested."

The old woman was soon snoring, and Jürgen thought a full grown bear might be quieter. He tidied up her cottage a bit, but did his best to leave most things where they were. He had his own way of organizing things and suspected she did, as well.

It was going on twilight the first day of the New Year when he went out to see about his horse. That sturdy fellow was doing well in the barn, enjoying the company of a cow and another horse, both hardy farm stock.

Jürgen patted his horse and then noticed a golden glow in the far stall. Curious, he went to the back and saw, half buried in the hay, several bags of gold coins and jewelry. Jürgen shook his head. If Anders had come here he would have surely taken every bag. Either he was off the Tinker's trail or the little thief was dead.

But not before dealing a nearly mortal blow, he thought, and his distaste for the bragging and oh-so-incompetent Tinker made him strike one of the barn's beams, startling the livestock.

"Sorry, my friends," he said, "I cry your pardon."

When he went back to the cottage the old woman was at the stove, preparing some soup.

"You should let me do that," he offered.

She waved him off with a large and ancient wooden

spoon.

"I've been making this stew since you were squalling in your crib, so don't get in my way, Huntsman."

He did as she bade and fetched some water from the well.

She set a steaming bowl before him, and the aroma was both tantalizing and strange. He looked at her, his eyebrows raised.

"It's not the Tinker, if that's what you're worried about, and it's not some lost brother and sister. It's venison, but the herbs change it a bit. Those I keep secret, if you don't mind, Jürgen von Vogt."

And so he ate, and it was the finest meal he had ever had, better than even dinner at the palace, he imagined.

After that, they talked, exchanging tales full of their love for the Black Forest and their adventures there.

She told him at last that her name was Elfriede, and that she had no surname, for she had been found in the woods as a child. When Jürgen asked her who found her, and who raised her, she merely smiled and told him that was a story for another time.

He began to suspect she might be the *Lutzelfrau*, after all.

#

Jürgen reported back to the Prince that Anders the Tinker had apparently fled the Black Forest. There was no trace of him anywhere and his usual cronies had not seen him since Christmas Eve. The Prince's representative wondered where he might have gone, and Jürgen suggested Britain or France, two nations ripe for a man of the Tinker's talents.

Elfriede soon grew strong enough to fend for herself, but Jürgen took to visiting her weekly. It was partly because he worried about her being all alone with so much gold so carelessly tucked away.

But the main truth was that he enjoyed her company.

On the subject of the gold, she told him not to worry, that she had never had any trouble. When he mentioned her recent misadventure, she laughed it off and said that it had been a blessing, for it had brought her a "most charming nursemaid."

At that he laughed and bowed, and she laughed, as well.

One day, he brought venison and some ale to share with Elfriede. He was surprised to find a young woman skinning a rabbit in the doorway, a bow and quiver of arrows at her side. She was about Jürgen's age with hair as black and lustrous as a starless night, and eyes as blue as a crisp, autumn sky. She wiped her brow and then smiled when she saw him.

"You must be Jürgen von Vogt," she said.

"I am."

"I am Hexe, and you have been caring for my aunt these last weeks. I thank you for that."

"Your aunt is a charming host. I am in her debt, actually."

"You're a man who does not make friends easily."

He smiled but said nothing.

"My aunt is asleep, poor old thing. Would you care to share some of your ale with me, Jürgen von Vogt?"

He nodded, then said, "I would just like to look in on her, if you don't mind."

She laughed, and he felt a shiver of pleasure travel down his spine at the sound of it. It was musical and pure, like water in a mountain stream.

"Auntie said you were cautious." She gestured at the door of the cottage. "Please."

Jürgen experienced a slight dizzy spell entering the cottage, but it passed quickly. And there was his dear old friend, fast asleep in her bed.

He went out to find Hexe had hung the rabbits in the smokehouse and was washing her hand in a small basin. She really was quite lovely.

Then she suddenly jumped on her horse and galloped away, daring him to catch her.

He did, but just barely.

For most of that year Jürgen divided his time between Hexe and her aunt. When the winds of October were heralding the coming winter, he knew he was in love with the young woman, who had no family outside of Elfriede.

When the first snows came, he went to the old woman.

"Greetings, Jürgen von Vogt," she said when he entered.

"Good day to you, Elfriede von Schwarzwald." He had taken to calling her this when formality was called for, and he could tell she delighted in it.

"You look odd," she said, studying his face. "Are you ill?"

"Nay. Nervous, yes; ill, no."

"I have never known anything to make you anxious, my friend – what is it that plagues you this day?"

"I have come to ask Hexe to be my bride."

Elfriede nodded gravely. "And you fear she will reject you?"

"I fear you may do so."

Elfriede nodded again.

"Shall I tell you something about my niece?" she asked quietly.

"That you are one in the same person?" he replied.

She smiled, and wagged a gnarled finger at him. "There are dangers to be had when spending time with a tracker and pathfinder!"

Jürgen said nothing.

"And so you have found out my secret – at least one of them – so many men would cry witchcraft and perhaps even wish to see me burned."

"I would sooner cut off my arms than see you come to harm, Elfriede."

"And you do not fear you have been courting an old crone all along?"

"My friend Helmut once told me that time is not so much a river as an aqueduct we travel upon. Were we better navigators, we might revisit those earlier aspects of ourselves, or even view our dotage and beyond."

"And if I told you that you were wrong, and that you have been fooled?"

Jürgen shrugged. "I have been alone all my life, Elfriede. If you will no more be Hexe to test my affections, then I will happily spend my days with you."

She laughed. "You are a sweet man, Jürgen von Vogt, but you do not understand." She whirled, and before him stood the beauty he had fallen in love with.

"This is my true form," she said, "that of Elfriede is for those seeking knowledge, or aid, or those who are in need of some lesson in humility, or honesty, or compassion."

Jürgen bowed before her, then sank to one knee. "Will you marry me, then, Hexe? Will you consent to spend your days with me until I am old and toothless?"

She laughed and pulled him up. "I will marry you, Jürgen von Vogt, and you best be certain of this course, for on our wedding day you will cease to age."

He kissed her, then fingered the ugly scar that marked his face like a stretch of troublesome road.

She slapped his hand away. "I will not alter your face, my beloved! Your scar was nobly won and marks you as a man of honor. Would I erase such a tribute?"

He had no words for that, so he kissed her again.

And that is how, in Christmas of that year, the long years of loneliness ended for Jürgen the Huntsman and Hexe the Yule Witch, and their long life together began.

And did they have many adventures, and do they live there, still.

Aye, but those are tales for another time.

Happy Christmas!

THE FIRST CHRISTMAS

Anno Domini One.

Some day it would be called the first Christmas, but that would not be for many years, yet.

In a small village a baby was born in the most humble of circumstances.

And while a baby is usually seen as a blessing, there were those who had heard of its birth and dreaded it.

They had seen the signs and portents, they had read the stars and charted the anomalies.

Theirs was a group without name. Indeed, mere words could not convey the evil they embraced, the chaos they pursued like ardent lovers.

To them the baby was nothing, but the man he would become... Ah, that would change everything.

And that was not something they could allow.

So they met in one of the old strongholds, far from prying eyes. They discussed and argued, debating their coming enemy for long hours into the night, settling at last on sending an assassin to remove their problem from the world.

But try as they might, using every spell and incantation known for the locating of enemies, they were unable to discern just where the child might be found.

All their prognostications showed that they must strike that night, the night of the child's birth, lest all be lost.

And so they went to the forbidden lore, the scrolls deemed far too dangerous for the eyes of men... And they found what they were looking for.

A being older than the world itself. A creature born outside of time and space, with a heart and soul like diseased and infested fruit, and an insatiable hunger for misery. The creature they sought had been imprisoned by Solomon under a great rock nearly a thousand years before, a great seal incised in the stone to keep the demon trapped.

Certain there was no other way, the enemies of the child went to that cursed place, and used their magick to remove the protective seal, to unlock the prison of stone.

The ancient words from the forbidden text were spoken, the winds ceased, and there was only silence.

The cabal looked at one another, nervously. It was only a few hours to dawn and then they would be undone. Then suddenly, a loud ringing sounded, as metal cleaved stone. The very earth split asunder, and their assassin crawled up out of the pit, vile and odious.

Cindaar kel Glaash, The Loathsome One.

He stood, nine feet tall and weighing nearly five hundred pounds.

His eyes flickered and burned like coals, but with a witch light of green and yellow. His nose was flattened and sported three nostrils. From his large mouth projected large tusks, some broken and jagged, the others filed to the sharpness of knives.

His skin was mottled and scaly, and cruel horns of obsidian rose from his temples and razor-like projections of bone and rock marched down his back.

He wore armor with a simple device, a red eye surrounded by a field of black, fealty to The Abyss.

In his massive and gnarled hands he carried a great axe, the very weapon he had used to split the stones that had held him place since the world was new.

He killed all of the sorcerers save one, the one who had had the presence to form a circle of protection around himself. He told the demon who to look for and commanded that he go forth.

Cindaar kel Glaash, his great axe dripping with gore, sniffed the air, once, twice, three times.

And then he smelled his prey.

The scent was maddening and stung his nose.

Cindaar kel Glaash hefted his axe toward the remaining sorcerer and grunted, then moved off at a trot, his taloned feet moving easily over rock and sand.

The survivor of that wretched group realized he had given

no command for when the child was dispatched, and decided the chaos and murder unleashed was precisely what they had wanted, all along. He left his circle of protection and went back to town, to tell the others of the cabal that the deed was done.

The demon traveled many miles to the village of Nazareth and moved unerringly past inns and homes to a stable. The hour was late and those who had come to pay homage to the child were gone or asleep.

The scent of the child was an anathema to him, irritating like a stinging insect inside his nose. It was maddening and he meant to end this annoyance now. He burst through the wooden door without pausing, stout timbers in the frame splintered like kindling, and he knocked aside the man who rushed to stop him.

A woman sat by a small bundle lying in the hay. Cindaar kel Glaash saw fear in her eyes, but she did not cry out or run.

And then he looked down at the child, and felt the armor of his evil blasted away - instantly.

The child gurgled and reached out to him, as if he were no more than a doting uncle, or a friendly shopkeeper. He, whom Solomon had called "He Who Defiles All He Touches."

Cindaar kel Glaash drew back, as a wave of goodness, of innocence, washed over him like a tide. To one such as him, it was pain beyond imagining. He cried out, dropping his great axe as he stumbled, half blind from the stable, out into the desert.

He wandered like that for many days, his body and mind wracked with agony.

He finally came to a cave overlooking a small settlement and crawled inside. He was raw and in pain, literally wasting away. He sloughed off his scaled, reptilian hide and the sand and stones ground into his raw flesh as vermin fed on him. His formidable height was now less than eight feet, his weight dwindling.

Cindaar kel Glaash languished in that cave for years, his bellows of pain causing the locals to fear that the place was haunted by an evil and hungry ghost.

Though he was immortal and could not die, he could suffer, and even a demon must take nourishment and water. So he starved, his throat parched to paper dryness, his body riddled with sores and open wounds, as his bones realigned themselves. The cave floor was littered with shards of obsidian and bone, the remnants of his great horns and dorsal spines.

His great tusks rotted and dropped out, fit for nothing more than an ugly necklace, now.

A girl, no more than seven, chanced upon him one day while looking for a lost kid from her family's goat herd. Her name was Esther and she held little truck with the stories of the "Haunted Cave."

By now, Cindaar kel Glaash looked like Goliath must have looked after being slain by David. He was hellishly ugly and still overly large, but he had lost most of his demonic aspect.

Esther gave him water, and the taste of it was so good, so remarkable in its healing power, that he quite forgot he used to eat children a millennium ago.

She brought him water and bits of goat meat, and put a poultice on the eye that had taken in most of the child's all-embracing goodness.

Cindaar kel Glaash did not fully heal, but he grew stronger. Now he was the size of a large man, a giant no longer, and white hair sprouted in place of cruel horns.

She asked him his name, but was unable to pronounce it. She decided just to call him "uncle," and he found himself absurdly pleased by that simple term.

There came a day when Esther's youngest brother went missing, and Cindaar kel Glaash found he could see the child, even though his vision was impeded by rock and distance. When Esther was reunited with her brother, her joy suffused him with a happiness he had never known, further healing him like a balm...

He began to do other small things, little things, tiny kindnesses.

Always in secret, for he was not used to communing with humans.

Fixing a wagon, mending a pen. He was quite good with his hands which had lost their talons and desire to take up killing weapons and instruments of cruelty.

He heard about the child he had been sent to slay, how he had grown to manhood only to be cruelly killed by men, and the news made him feel something else he had never felt.

Sadness.

So Cindaar kel Glaash redoubled his efforts, doing good acts, and finding with delight that some of his magick remained, and aided him in his deeds and gifts.

One day, when Esther was very old, he told her he was going away. He had an idea how he might bring hope to the world and honor the child who had brought about such a miraculous transformation in him, and perhaps all of Mankind.

And Esther said, "Uncle, you once told me your name and I could not pronounce it - I would hear it, one last time."

And Cindaar kel Glaash, who had not thought of his name in many years, found he could not form those sounds either, so he adopted the strange and melodious version that escaped his lips that day:

Santa Claus.

THE THREE

It was 6 p.m. on Christmas Eve, and the Barman was ready for the usual collection of revelers, lost causes and unclaimed souls that would wander in and have to be shooed out at closing. In his five years tending bar at the Four Crowns, he figured he had seen every type you could imagine, from every country on Earth.

So when the Gaunt Man walked in, he was a little taken aback. The newcomer was tall, easily two meters, but couldn't have weighed more than six or seven stone. The Gaunt man was dressed in threadbare pants and a black hoodie, the hood pulled low enough to obscure most of his face.

The Barman wondered if this might be a robbery, and wished the fellow well, because he had a cudgel under the bar that had been a gift from his great uncle in Dublin.

Besides, what sort of person robs a pub on Christmas Eve?

The Gaunt Man approached the bar, and the Barman detected a wheeze. The Gaunt Man placed a very bony hand upon the bar as if to steady himself.

A good bartender knows when to keep his mouth shut, and you never addressed a fellow's looks or his infirmity. If they wanted to share what was ailing them, they would let you know soon enough.

"Happy Christmas to you, sir, what can I get you?" the Barman asked politely.

The Barman had set up candles to make the place more festive, and an occasional flicker seemed to hint at a large grin underneath the hoodie.

The Gaunt Man pointed to a bottle of single malt.

The Barman retrieved the bottle. "This, then?" he asked, wanting to make sure.

The slightest inclination of the hood. A nod, then.

The Barman poured the Gaunt Man two fingers of scotch, then looked at him.

A bony finger pointed to the top of the glass.

The Barman filled it, and the Gaunt Man put a coin down on the counter. As the Barman was picking it up, the Gaunt Man took his drink and the bottle to a booth far in back, where even bright lights or sunshine never seemed to penetrate.

The Barman looked at the coin, which was a gold sovereign from 1843. That had to be far too much! Sure, it was Christmas, but a coin like this must be worth a hundred pounds or more.

Perhaps the Gaunt Man was a rich eccentric, or perhaps he meant to pay for several rounds with friends not yet arrived.

Deciding they could settle up when the Gaunt Man was leaving, the Barman put the coin in a special compartment near the register where he kept large bills and once, a diamond engagement ring.

Shaking his head, the Barman wondered if the coin might bring enough for him to buy his girl that dress she had wanted.

In the back, the Gaunt Man drank his scotch in silence.

Outside, the entire transaction had been witnessed by the Laughing Man and the Pale Girl.

The Laughing Man was tall, though not as tall as the Gaunt Man, but he was of an enormous girth, weighing easily twenty-four stone. He had bright red hair, a full beard, and a mustache that curled up at the ends quite on their own. He was dressed in a simple suit and a top coat with a fur collar. He carried a walking stick with a boar's head on the handle. On his head was a bowler hat with a sprig of mistletoe in the band.

The Pale Girl was seven or eight, and quite lovely. Her hair was such a pale blonde as to be nearly white, and her eyes were the solemn gray of an overcast sea. She was dressed in a pale blue velvet dress and a tiny top coat that had a sprig of holly on the lapel. In one pale hand was a small valise.

The Laughing Man frowned, something he did not do often. "I say, has he been here every night?" His voice was pleasant baritone, one suitable for announcers and radio personalities.

"Different bars, but always in the back, where it's darkest."

"Alone?"

She nodded. "For over a week now," she said. Her voice was soft but mellifluous, the sort of voice an angel might have.

The Laughing Man shook his head, not at all happy. "If something is troubling him, why not come to us?"

"Perhaps he is too proud," said the Pale Girl. "Perhaps he is afraid."

"Him? Afraid?" Now the Laughing Man did laugh, a hearty, booming guffaw that caused passers-by to laugh and wave.

The Laughing Man tipped his hat to them and then bent down to the Pale Girl. "How can he be afraid? He is Fear Incarnate… He is the Rider of the Night-Mare."

The Pale Girl looked up at him, and nodded. "But we are his family, and so we have a special place in his heart, a spot where fear might yet reside… And sadness."

"But what is he sad about, what ails him?" asked the Laughing Man.

But, instead of answering, the Pale Girl was heading into the bar, and the Laughing Man had to hurry to catch up.

# #

The Gaunt Man did not look up when the Laughing Man and the Pale Girl entered the bar. He had known the minute they began peering at him through the window.

It didn't make him angry. In truth, nothing could penetrate this miasma of sadness that had settled on him like a pernicious fog.

The Barman point to the Pale Girl while addressing the Laughing Man. "No kids allowed in this establishment, sir."

The Laughing Man turned to the bar in a motion that was quick and surprisingly nimble for one of his size. He motioned the Barman to come closer with a conspiratorial gesture.

The Barman drew close, and the Laughing Man lowered his voice. "That's my brother," he said in what seemed genuine sadness, "and that's his little girl, my niece. We are trying to get him to come home for Christmas. I thought she might be more persuasive, you see, and -- "

The Barman nodded. "Just make it quick - I don't want to be sacked on Christmas Eve."

The Laughing Man nodded and then produced a coin with a flourish. "For your trouble."

As the two walked toward the back, the Barman looked at the coin.

Gold sovereign, 1843.

Now he was a bit worried. What if these coins were stolen, perhaps from rich collector with ties to the police and the mayor?

But if they were, wouldn't they have just spent regular money, or wanted change? And him letting a family talk on Christmas Eve was hardly worth a hundred or so pounds.

The Laughing Man and the Pale Girl sat opposite the Gaunt Man. Normally no one would be able to sit next to the Laughing Man in such a small space, but he did not have his great coat on, and the Pale Girl was no larger than a wisp.

The Gaunt Man raised his glass in an ironic toast, and drained it.

The Pale Girl tugged on the Laughing Man's sleeve and he inclined his head. She whispered in his ear and he listened, then went pale.

"Emily says you want to quit," the Laughing Man said, gesturing to the Pale Girl. It was not her real name. They had been in their respective positions so long they had forgotten their true names. The Pale Girl had decided that she liked the sound of Emily, at least for now, and had asked that they call her that when it was just the three. Doting on her as they always did, they let her christen them Uncle Marble-Towne (the Gaunt Man) and Uncle Greathorn (the Laughing Man).

"It's true, isn't it, Uncle Marble-Towne?" she asked, her tiny forehead suddenly lined with worry wrinkles.

The Gaunt Man sighed and the temperature in the bar plummeted ten degrees. Several patrons gathered their coats tighter around them and the Barman checked the thermostat.

"But, surely you know you can't quit," protested the Laughing Man. "If you go, none of it works and we shall all be in peril."

"Un…happy," the Gaunt Man wheezed, and a mouse under the table with a crust of bread became so despondent it rushed home to check on its family, leaving the choice morsel behind. The Gaunt Man reached for his bottle, but it was empty. He motioned to the Barman, but that good fellow was too busy seeing to a group of students who were ushering in their Christmas with spirits.

The Gaunt Man excused himself and went to fetch another bottle. Liquor had little effect on him and his gait was unimpeded, save for the fact that his hooded head hung low.

The Laughing Man shook his head. "What will the August Company say?" he asked worriedly, "and what about The Author?"

The Pale Girl patted the Laughing Man's ruddy face. "It's all right," she said, smiling sweetly, "I have an idea."

"What sort of idea, my dear?"

"You and I are going to give him a Christmas gift."

"But he doesn't need anything."

"Doesn't he?" she asked, and smiled.

The Gaunt Man returned with his bottle and a glass for the Laughing Man. He also had a hot cocoa for the Pale Girl, who sipped it gratefully. She wiped some whipped cream from the end of her nose and regarded her gaunt uncle with solemnity.

"You're tired of being the Gaunt Man, aren't you?"

There was a long pause, and then the Gaunt Man nodded.

"You'd like a try at something else... Perhaps something cheerier?"

Now he looked at them, and his eyes burned like coals. Any mortal would have been afraid, but there were none such in that little booth that night.

"But he *is* the Gaunt Man," the Laughing Man protested. "He always has been."

"But nothing says he has to be," the Pale Girl said. "There's nothing that says we can't trade off."

The two adults looked at her, thunderstruck. It was an idea that might only occur to a child, and its wisdom and simplicity were as sublime as the pearlescent gray of her eyes.

The Laughing Man slowly grinned, then laughed a great laugh. The candles in the bar burned more merrily and the Barman discovered to his shock that the far end of the bar was suddenly laden with a lavish Christmas feast. He called his girlfriend as the patrons began to help themselves.

In the rear of the Four Crowns, the Three regarded one another. A moment of wordless communication passed, and then they nodded.

The Barman looked up as they left. He had meant to bring up the coins, but thought perhaps he had imagined them, for here the patrons from the back were leaving, and they seemed so very different from what he remembered. In front was a pale boy with red hair. Behind him came an immensely large man with blonde hair and beard, looking like something out of Norse mythology. And bringing up the rear was a tall woman, impossibly old and gaunt, her hooded cloak pulled tight around her, her face in shadow.

"Happy Christmas," the Barman called, and the Gaunt Woman tossed him his third gold sovereign.

And, as the revelers of the Four Crowns began to sing of Good King Wenceslas, the ghosts of Christmas Past, Present and Future went out into the night.

HOME FOR THE HOLIDAYS, REVISITED

The fire was burning low as James Chesterton, their jovial host, turned to Charlie.

In the flickering light of candles and embers he looked more like Fezziwig than ever, and Charlie wondered if he might have fallen asleep during some Dickens production on cable.

"The last tale of the evening falls to you, my young friend," said Chesterton with an expansive gesture.

Charlie had declined several times that evening. Now the fire was burning low and they turned to him expectantly. Rebecca gave him an encouraging smile.

The truth was, he hated talking in front of a group of strangers. Others seemed to find it so easy, but his heart would always hammer and his voice would falter. And the only tales he could recall were synopses of various Christmas specials he had seen as a child. That hardly seemed to be what was called for -

here.

Charlie looked at their host, put out his empty hands

look, no stories here!

and shook his head. "Sorry," he said.

Their host smiled, but there was a hint of anger in it, of rudeness perceived and not entirely forgiven.

"I have another one," ventured Rebecca, "I can go for him."

Chesterton raised his hand. "Not necessary, my dear, no one should be forced to sing for his supper." Although Charlie thought that was exactly what the man believed.

The big man surveyed a clock on the mantle. "It is late, my friends, and tomorrow we shall have a most splendid Christmas. I wish you all sweet slumber and pleasant dreams."

In their room, he and Rebecca tried their cells again, to no avail.

"Tomorrow the costumes will be off and we'll get word to your folks," Charlie promised her.

No valet or chamber maid came to see to their undressing, which was fine by Charlie. He had quite enough of the eighteenth century.

Rebecca seemed troubled, and he pulled her close as they wiggled under the covers.

"You okay?"

"I just wish... You're a good story teller, Charlie, I wish you had told them something, anything."

"You know I'm no good at public speaking, Beck. Besides, Fezziwig didn't really care."

"Don't call him that," she said in a whisper, "and I think he does care, very much."

Charlie put his arms around her and kissed her. "I'll apologize properly tomorrow, and we'll send him a nice bottle of wine for his hospitality."

She nodded and he kissed her nose, then her mouth.

"I love you, Beck."

"I love you, too," she said. She started to say something, but shut her mouth.

"What?"

"Nothing. I love you very much, Charlie."

He nodded, smiling, and they blew out the candles.

The bed was luxurious and comfortable, even though the blizzard howled outside. Charlie felt Rebecca in his arms, soft and warm.

"Merry Christmas," he whispered, and fell asleep.

# #

Charlie awoke, shivering from the cold, his back and legs aching from being cramped.

He straightened, his back protesting, and found himself on a moth-eaten couch, stained and falling apart, clearly a nesting place for mice and other vermin.

He looked around him, at the great room now gone to mildew and rot, the great fireplace broken and empty save for ashes and beer cans.

The great chandelier was gone, and the moldy wallpaper hung in strips like leprous flesh.

"Beck? Rebecca?" His voice echoed in the cavernous space, small and lonely.

He looked for her, but there was no sign of her, their hosts or any of the guests from last night. He wondered if he had been drugged, his mind spinning out wild scenarios of a waitress at their last diner stop slipping him a drug while Rebecca was kidnapped.

He was dressed in his regular clothes although his shirt was on backwards.

He stumbled out of the great room to find the large staircase lying in charred rubble, the second story burned long ago and the absent roof making way for rot and pigeons over what looked like decades.

Centuries, even

That was absurd. He had been here last night, they both had, and they ate fine food and danced and told stories.

Well, he had listened to stories.

The downstairs was deserted, stripped of furnishings and decor long ago, the fine tapestries and paintings replaced with obscene graffiti and holes punched or kicked in the walls.

He went to the front and found it boarded up with plywood, but this had been worked by vandals until one need only push on a side to gain access or egress.

It was a beautiful winter day outside, the sun shining in a

crisp, blue sky with just a smattering of white clouds. He made his way back to the car and was not quite surprised to find it started right up.

As he was searching for his cell, something in his pocket crinkled.

He pulled out a sheet of very fine linen paper that looked ancient.

I'm sorry

That's all it said, but he knew Rebecca's handwriting well enough.

He got out of the car with the note, and an errant breeze tugged at it. Charlie held onto it, but it disintegrated like ashes in his hand, blowing over the hedge like gray snowflakes. He heard gay music from the house, music from long ago, and peeked around the hedge.

The house looked whole again, just for a moment, and he saw Rebecca standing at the window. She was wearing a different dress, one as fine as the night before. She mimed that she loved him, and then the house seemed to shrink and fade, until it was the ruin he had left earlier.

He reeled at the loss of her, and could his mind wanting to deny it all, to shut down and seek solace in some fantasy.

No.

He had gotten himself in this predicament, and felt Rebecca's goodbye was a hint that he might make things right.

He wrote down the house's position on the GPS, which seemed to be functioning all right again.

Charlie knew there were difficult times ahead. He would have to deal with a lot of tough questions, and being alone.

But he would prevail, and he would come back... Every Christmas Eve for the rest of his life, if necessary.

And he would have a story ready.

ABOUT THE AUTHOR

Mark Onspaugh grew up in the San Fernando Valley of Los Angeles, California. His father, writer and aeronautical engineer Carl Onspaugh, was a fan of science fiction and Mark visited many strange and wonderful places, thanks to editors like Judith Merril and Groff Conklin. Besides his father he counts Ray Bradbury, Robert Sheckley, Robert Bloch and Eric Frank Russell among his early influences. A proud member of the Horror Writers Association, he lives in Cambria, California with his wife, writer Tobey Crockett PhD.

Printed in Great Britain
by Amazon.co.uk, Ltd.,
Marston Gate.